THE RECKLESS APPRENTICE

Cover designed by Deranged Doctor Design

HE Scott
Visit my website at www.hescott.ca

Printed in the United States of America

ISBN-978-0-9921475-1-8

The Reckless Apprentice

Chronicles of Sangan
Book 1

H.E. Scott

For Jim,

Thank you for your faith in me and all the little nudges along the way.

"The only way around is through." Robert Frost

Table of Contents

CHAPTER 1

Huddled on the floor of a dingy room, his back pressed tightly against the wall, a scruffy man wrapped his arms tightly around his knees. His hand shook as he pushed a strand of greasy hair off his face.

On the other side of the room a woman and two men sat at a grimy table, revulsion etched on their faces. The woman held a sachet filled with aromatic spices to her nostrils and stared malevolently down at the man sitting on the floor.

The man fidgeted uneasily, avoiding her gaze by concentrating on the men's rich, leather boots. Men of their status never associated with the lower classes, especially one of the nameless men, a gong farmer. Gong farmers spent their lives underground, cleaning the sewers.

The greasy-haired man, fearfully eyed the assembled group, “The first stage has gone well, Master,” he mumbled. As a gong farmer, he was well acquainted with the city’s sewers and underground tunnels. For that knowledge alone they chose Jacq, the skinny, gong farmer to smuggle banned weapons into the castle, under the noses of the castle guards.

“You keep your opinions to yourself,” snarled Girard, the larger of the two men. "You had a simple task, to bring all the swords here, not leave one out in the open for someone to find.”

Jacq glanced at a leather sack, crusted with wet sand, lying beside the table, the hilts of five swords sticking out the opening. “But master, I have taken care of the problem. No one will find it or the corpse," whined Jacq, his voice high-pitched and fearful.

"I have hidden them well. There will be nothing recognizable. The crawlers..."

“Be silent,” roared Girard, slamming his fist hard onto the table. The gong farmer jerked his head back in shock, bumping it on the wall.

Nervously, Jacq edged his way closer to the door as his thoughts turned to the events of the previous evening. The leather sack with the swords had split open as he dragged it across the beach. One gleaming hilt protruded from the sack. Temptation proved too great. He pulled it from the sack and from its scabbard. He swung the blade back and forth, imagining himself brandishing the blade in a fight. How could he have known a soldier coming from the castle watched him?

Jacq buried the sword and the body, hiding all traces of blood from the soldier’s deadly wounds. Bile rose in his throat as he remembered the dead weight and staring eyes of the corpse as he pushed it into the hole. He wiped his dirty sleeve across his mouth, leaving a smear of grime across his cheek and started to shake uncontrollably, not because of the dead man but the lost weapon and his fear of Girard. Just then another man entered the room, leaving the door ajar. Jacq quickly slipped through the opening and disappeared down the dark tunnels, mistaken in his belief he went unnoticed.

"Find the vermin," said Girard, giving a nod to the new arrival. The man put his hand to his chest in salute then silently exited the room.

Jacq, ran as fast as he could down a short tunnel then through a door into the sewers, a place he had called home all his life. He knew the sewers well. He required no torch to see where he was going, running, when he could, on the small ledge bordering each side of the rank tunnel, at times through the sewer's foul contents.

The screech of rusty, metal hinges, told Jacq someone pursued him. He glanced back over his shoulder and saw the flare of a torch. Sweat ran cold down his back when he heard the footsteps of his pursuer echoing on the tunnel walls. He had no choice but to go on.

At a fork in the tunnel, he stopped to listen. The footsteps continued, one, two, three, then they stopped. He knew the man was closing in or perhaps it was the woman pursuing him. Jacq didn't know why she was at the meeting with Girard; he only knew she frightened him more than the men did. She wore a scowl on her face that seemed carved there permanently. Whoever it was, he could not afford to wait and find out.

The next tunnel turned back, angling towards the castle. He hurried down that tunnel where he knew it ended at a small, barred gate. He knew that nearby where the tunnels forked, a ladder hung in an alcove on his left side. If only he could reach it before his pursuer caught up to him.

Jacq dragged his fingers along the slimy wall, searching for the alcove and the ladder, his only way of escape. Finally, his hand slipped into empty space. Almost giddy with relief he climbed the rusty ladder, trusting it would bear his weight, as the splashing footsteps of his pursuer approached. The footsteps slowed, then stopped.

Frightened, Jacq held his breath, believing his breathing and maybe even the pounding of his heart would reveal him, clinging to the rusty ladder. The man stopped for only a moment and then his splashing footsteps drew away into the blackness of the tunnel.

Jacq took a shallow breath of the fetid air. He did not have much time. The tunnel below ended maybe fifty feet further. When the footsteps grew faint, he began to climb the rest of the way up the ladder but slipped, and smashed his nose on a rung. His eyes teared with pain. He wanted to scream.

Regaining his grip on the ladder he climbed to the top and fumbled for the latch on the trapdoor above his head. When he found the latch, he stood motionless for a moment, listening for movement below. Hearing nothing, he pulled on the latch, praying to the Goddess for the downtrodden to help him escape his wretched life. He yanked again and again but the latch, seized from years of disuse, barely moved. Frantically, he wiggled it back and forth, until it slid with a loud, rasping noise in time with the echoing steps of his pursuer's return.

He flung the hatch open and slid his smelly, slime-covered body through. At the same moment, a knife flew through the opening, clattering harmlessly against the wall. Jacq slammed the trapdoor and fell upon it, hoping his weight would keep his pursuer from opening the door.

The person on the other side of the trapdoor pushed and pushed but Jacq stayed firmly lying upon it. When the man finally gave up, Jacq remained there, exhausted. He sent another prayer to the Goddess in thanks, again beseeching her to help him escape his wretched life.

Jacq did not doubt his pursuer went away to get help. It wouldn't take long for them to return. He knew his fate loomed very near. Even his full weight on the door would not be enough to keep it closed if more than one man pushed from below. Even though Jacq had no light to see he knew the room was one of the gong rooms where he removed night soil and carted it to the fields. He dragged his fingers along the wall, in search of the door leading into the tunnels and temporary safety. When he found the door, Jacq let out the breath he didn't realize he was holding. He opened the door a crack and peeked out. Seeing no one working nearby, he exited the room and searched for a shovel to wedge against the door. At the least, no one could follow him from that direction.

Safe, for the moment, Jacq leaned against the wall and slowly slid down until he sat on the cold, stone floor. As his pounding heart slowed and he could stand, without shaking, Jacq stealthily crept through the lower passageways of the castle in search of somewhere to hide. He needed to rest, to think how he could get himself out of this mess. He carried his despair like a cold ball in his stomach. He could not go back to his hovel. He had nowhere to go. He was homeless.

Chapter 2

Nada closed her eyes and rested her head on the driftwood stump behind her. The sun warmed her face and the sea breeze ruffled her hair, but she couldn't relax. Usually, sitting in her favorite spot, looking out to sea would have calmed her. But this day, anger and disappointment overwhelmed her.

This day was her day. Reaching maturity and celebrating a naming day should be a grand celebration. Nada expected just a small celebration with friends and had arisen earlier than usual, happy with the world. When her mother announced they would have a small, quiet celebration, just the two of them, Nada stomped out of their chamber, slamming the door behind her.

“Arrrggh,” she growled, allowing herself to succumb to the anger she felt. She kicked at the ground, stomping and pushing her feet further down under the sand where it was cool and damp. Suddenly a searing pain shot through her foot and up her leg. Nada gasped in shock, jerked her foot back and squeezed it tightly with both hands. Tears welled up in her eyes as blood streamed between her fingers, leaving a crimson puddle on the sand. Her heart pounded, and her stomach clenched, threatening to disgorge her breakfast. The bile rose quickly, almost choking her. She breathed deeply, slowly; attempting to stop the nausea she always felt at the sight of blood. It was not just the blood causing her reaction but the fear of poisonous shellfish that inhabited the waters nearby. Big, strong men, could succumb to very small injuries from shellfish poison.

Nada couldn't bring herself to look at the wound. She knew it was no small scratch from the amount of blood and the throbbing pain in her foot. Hastily, she pulled herself up, using the stump for balance. By hopping and stumbling she crossed the beach to the cobbled roadway leading to a small service entrance of Castle Pelagos. She stumbled many times and left a trail of blood to mark her path.

A silly thought came to her. She was supposed to be helping in the kitchen this day. She imagined Aldred, the cook, slamming her huge stirring spoon down on her work counter, mumbling she was good for nothing. The thought of Aldred being angry spurred her on.

Some children playing nearby stopped to watch Nada's wild hopping. They laughed at the sight. Her hair straggled crazily in front of her face. She looked like one of the beggar children who scavenged along the beaches, wild and unkempt. With a strange grimace, she toppled and fell face first, expelling her breath with a grunt as she landed in a puff of dust. The smaller children all screamed in unison, "Nada's dead." They displayed no emotion, just a mass exclamation as if the sight of someone falling face first in the dirt was commonplace.

Hearing the children screaming outside, Aldred lifted her heavy body from her chair to investigate. She appeared to move in slow motion as all the huge parts of her body responded. Her breasts wobbled and jiggled in time with her massive legs and bottom. When she arrived outside, she saw the children standing in a circle around Nada's motionless body. Aldred's mouth gaped at the sight of her favorite helper lying in the dirt, with a huge, bloody gash running the length of her foot. Nada's eyes were open and staring; spittle bubbles on her lips the only sign she still breathed.

Aldred grabbed the nearest boy roughly by his arm, squeezing it painfully. "Run, tell healer, Elieana, that Nada is hurt, and I am bringing her to their chamber."

Aldred knew poison caused Nada's symptoms but held her tongue, not wanting to sound an alarm. She gave the boy a shove to send him on his way. Another boy, she sent to the kitchen, to fetch a kettle of boiled water. She heaved Nada's body up into her arms and carried her to the large chamber she shared with her mother, Elieana.

Philen, a boy of the same age as Nada, stood frozen at the sight of his best friend with foam spilling from her mouth. Aldred growled at Philen as she passed. "Instead of taking root there, boy, find out what caused this gash on her foot."

Philen nodded and followed the bloody trail. He found where Nada fell once or twice; in those places little pools blood congealed in the hot sun. Using the toe of his boot he flipped sand over the spots to chase the insects off. He followed the bloody trail to a large, wind worn, driftwood stump.

Philen could see nothing sharp sticking up from the sand that could cut someone so drastically. Thinking it must be a poisonous shell he picked up a stick and pushed it down into the sand to dislodge whatever might be buried there. Immediately he struck something hard. He dug with the stick and uncovered the hilt of a sword, buried just beneath the surface. Philen grasped the hilt and pulled it free. The carved hilt and basket told the tale of what it was not. It was not a soldier's sword. The cruel looking blade was sharpened on both sides, two hands in length, narrowed at the hilt and widening out to a curving point. Brownish-green crystals coated the blade of the assassin's sword he held in his hand.

Philen's fear for Nada intensified. He had learned enough from the soldiers and his father to know that poison caused Nada's violent symptoms. Shellfish poison did not cause someone to react the way Nada did, this was something more sinister. He pulled off his vest, wrapped it around the sword and carried it gingerly back to the castle to search out Jorian, one of the King's officers and a friend of his father.

The massive door to the officer's quarters opened smoothly on freshly oiled hinges. A puff of air wafted through the doorway, cool compared to the heat of the day outside. It took a moment for Philen's eyes to adjust to the torch light in the passageway. He trod lightly on the flagstone floor, not wanting to announce his presence. Darec Redford, newly arrived at the castle, Captain of the King's Guard, did not welcome unescorted people. A shiver of dread shook Philen's body, from the sense of urgency of his task but also from the thought of encountering Darec. He sped up, his boot heels clomping loudly on the flagstones, as he ran towards Jorian's apartment at the end of the passageway.

The click of a latch startled him, and he quickened his pace. He rapped loudly when he reached Jorian's door. At the same time, Darec Redford exited his apartment, his body seeming to block the light of the torches hanging on the wall behind him.

Darec wore reddish colored boots; tight fitting leggings; a loose-fitting tunic, laced at the neck and a leather jerkin cinched tight with a wide leather belt. A knife sheath hung from Darec's belt. Gossips around the castle said Darec took the blade off a dead soldier during the war between Pelagonia and Baltica, Pelagonia's neighbor to the south. The stories the gossips told of how he used the knife on the enemy were frightening.

With the torchlight behind him, Darec's face remained in shadow but Philen could see his jaw clenching tightly as he ground his teeth. A cold sneer spread across Darec's face. Just as Darec opened his mouth to growl at Philen. Jorian opened the door and Philen scrambled inside. Jorian leaned out of the doorway, looked at Darec, then shrugged his shoulders. With a half-hidden smile, Jorian followed Philen into the room; not waiting to hear what Darec was about to say. Jorian knew of the hostility Darec held toward young people, Philen being no exception.

Jorian waited while Philen stumbled over his words, thinking the meeting with Darec probably caused Philen's difficulty. Frustrated with his failed attempts to speak Philen tore open the vest he carried. The weapon fell to the floor with a thud, shaking off some of the crystals coating the blade. Jorian knelt and grasped the hilt of the sword but then a queer expression spread across his face. Cautiously he laid the sword down on the floor, careful not to touch the blade. He stood up and turned to leave the room. "Stay where you are, Philen," he said over his shoulder. "Do not pick up the sword. Do not touch it. Drop your vest on the floor."

Obediently Philen dropped the vest and took a cautious step backward. Satisfied, Jorian exited the room. When he reached the courtyard, Jorian, saw Darec briskly walking toward the stables. "Darec!" Jorian called out loudly.

Darec stopped walking, his tension visible in the flexion of his shoulders. "What is it?" Said Darec.

"Come back to my apartment," said Jorian. "Philen brought something you should see. I know you will be interested."

"Tell me here. The child's playthings are no concern of mine. You deal with him if you want to. I have no use for children, they get in my way."

"If playthings had anything to do with why you should come back with me I would speak no further. You must overcome your loathing of children for the moment; an old enemy may be in our midst."

Darec's face paled under his ruddy complexion and he immediately turned back towards the officer's apartments. He pushed the door open with such force it slammed against the wall. The torches hanging on the wall flickered as he passed, and the sound of his boots echoed in the passageway as he covered the distance to Jorian's room.

Philen sat at the table in Jorian's apartment, his head resting on his arms. Finally, he allowed himself a moment to think of the danger to his friend, Nada. He feared the poison may have killed her. Meeting up with Darec didn't help. Philen could not understand why Darec despised him so much. For that matter, he did not know why Darec detested any of the young people in the castle. Never had any one of them done anything to earn such hatred.

Suddenly Darec stomped into the room. Philen jerked upright in the chair and briefly met Darec's gaze then he turned toward the door, gauging the distance for a quick escape. Darec ignored Philen and bent down to look at the sword, still laying where Jorian had placed it. Turning it carefully, Darec examined the hilt and the sickly green crystals on the blade. "It is one of Girard's; he or one of his men has carved his last handiwork into the hilt," said Darec.

"King Stephan, with his newly adopted son, soon arrives from Baltica. Perhaps Girard lays in wait for them or someone attending the treaty signing and marriage," said Jorian.

To make peace between the kingdoms of Baltica and Pelagonia, Princess Verenase of Pelagonia, daughter of King Albryk, would marry, Michael, the adopted son of King Stephan of Baltica. Michael's true father, Vasilis, brother to King Stephan's missing wife, Antonia, would also attend the marriage.

"Someone could be paying Girard well to stop the signing of the treaty; there are some who would profit from the continuation of war. I have not heard of any dispute to the marriage, but perhaps you are right. King Albryk will announce his guests soon. I will arrange to meet with him and his advisors, the answer may be written in the list," said Jorian.

"It is strange; Girard is not careless with his weapons. He would not leave a sword laying around for a child to find," said Darec.

"I don't think Girard is getting sloppy. Your order of no weapons in the city will have something to do with the sword being where Philen found it," said Jorian.

"Yes, perhaps you are right, Jorian. Send a man to the gate for a list of people who have entered the city. Perhaps the guards there will remember someone refusing to check their weapons."

Philen looked anxiously from one man to the other, shaking his head in disbelief. What did the royal wedding have to do with Nada's wound? Why did they talk of checking weapons at the gates? They were not talking about Nada and, more importantly, how they could help her. Philen leapt from his chair, knocking it backwards onto the floor. "What are you talking about?" he shouted. "Don't you know Nada has been cut and she's bleeding? Can you not see she needs help? Even I know poison covered the blade she slashed her foot on."

"This poison acts very fast. If your friend has even a small cut from this sword, unless someone gives her the antidote immediately, she will be dead," said Darec.

Darec spoke in such a matter-of-fact way it left Philen speechless. His eyes widened briefly, the only indication he heard and understood what Darec said. Philen's face paled but he did not show any other sign he could not cope with this news. He felt helpless. His shoulders slumped. He knew he must be strong, for Nada's sake. Perhaps, somehow, she had survived under the healer's care.

Darec realized his bluntness from the bloodless look on the boy's face. He had the antidote for this poison. He knew he was the only person in the castle who could help her. If she still lived. Darec's icy reserve melted slightly. He grasped Philen's shoulder, squeezing it gently, attempting to reassure him. "Tell me where she is," said Darec.

"Aldred took her to the healer's chamber. She is the healer's daughter," said Philen.

"All right, I will gather some things and meet you at the healer's chamber."

Bewildered by Darec's reassurance, but having no time to think on it, Philen ran out of the room.

Darec carefully picked up the sword, not touching it anywhere near the green crystals. He left the chamber with Jorian following closely behind him. "Jorian, you must make sure the floor is cleaned with lye and the clothing burned. We do not want to have another accident with this poison."

Jorian nodded, "I will take care of it, have no fear. I don't want to be the next victim by stepping on it with my bare feet."

"I think you may want to go and comfort the boy first, if the girl has died."

Leaving Jorian to continue to the healer's chamber Darec took the sword to his quarters. He entered his chamber and locked the door then he flipped back a rug in the middle of the room and pried up one of the floorboards with his knife. A small, intricately decorated, metal box lay inside. On the lid, carved in relief, a ruby-eyed snake coiled around a staff. The box contained a black leather pouch. Inside the pouch was a small metal cup; a vial of white powder; a vial of clear liquid and a thin piece of metal.

Darec scraped the green crystals from the sword into the metal cup, then sprinkled some of the white powder on top of the green crystals. The crystallized blood gradually turned pure white. What remained in the cup was the antidote for the poison. After he was finished he placed all the items, except the cup with the antidote and the vial of liquid back into the box and returned it to its hiding place. He tucked the sword in beside the box, then replaced the floorboard and the rug.

As he hurried to the healer's chamber, Darec prepared himself for the anguish in the room when he arrived. Without a doubt death had already paid a visit. A young girl, dead before she had a chance to live. He shook his head to shake away the thought then steeled his resolve for what he would find.

Jorian was waiting for Darec at the bottom of a winding stairway. They climbed the stairs and found the door to the healer's chamber ajar, giving the two men a chance to survey the large, comfortable room before entering. Thick carpets of blue, rust and brown, woven in unusual patterns, covered the floor. Lanterns cast a warm, golden glow. Shelves on the walls overflowed with books and scraps of paper. Books littered the top of a desk. A large cabinet with many tiny drawers, each with a different set of strange symbols on them, stood opposite the table. Darec recognized the cabinet as an apothecary cabinet, usually seen in the city of Belisle, capital of Baltica. Philen, sat on a chair by a sturdy, wooden table and nodded at the men as they entered.

On the other side of the room a drapery hung in front of a small alcove. Darec immediately noticed the absence of emotion in the room. Complete silence. He walked over and pulled the drapery aside, revealing a narrow bed upon which, Nada lay. Pale skin revealed her deathly illness but the slow rise and fall of her chest showed she still clung to life.

A woman, almost as tall as Darec, rose from a chair beside the bed and glared at him. "Who are you? What are you doing here?" she said.

Jorian stepped from behind Darec and her demeanor changed. "We came as soon as we could, Elieana. This is Darec Redford. He has knowledge of this poison and brought the antidote."

Elieana moved forward, blocking the men's entrance into the alcove. "Philen told me you were coming, Jorian. I have taken care of the wound; Nada will recover."

Darec slipped past Elieana and approached the bed. He took out the small cup of powdered antidote, poured some liquid on top, mixed it and then poured the liquid onto a clean cloth. Elieana pulled at Darec's arm, attempting to remove him from the alcove but he shrugged her hand away. "Woman, what are you trying to do?" he demanded rudely. "This girl is as good as dead, if I cannot apply the antidote."

Elieana stepped back, surprised at his forcefulness and watched as Darec gently lifted the blanket from Nada's foot. Again, Elieana pulled at Darec's arm, furiously raising her voice. "Jorian, take this man away. I do not need his help. Nada will be fine. I have taken care of her injury. We do not need his help." Elieana again tried to shove Darec off the chair but due to his size and strength, Elieana could not move him.

Gently Darec lifted Nada's leg to look at the wound on the sole of her foot. A physician's neat stitches closed the wound spanning the length of her foot. No crust of green crystals remained. Dumbstruck, Darec looked up at Elieana. The war in Baltica nearly claimed the physician's entire guild. He knew of only a very few physicians remaining alive. Some no longer used their skills, afraid to challenge the ban on healing practices and the very real fear of punishment by death for doing so. "Where did you acquire the knowledge to cure this poison?" he said very quietly. He turned back and looked at Nada's wound again, but his attention was diverted by a tiny, four-petaled, white flower tattooed just below Nada's ankle. He set Nada's foot down gently then turned to Elieana, his eyes narrowed to slits. "Who are you, woman," he said rudely. "And whose child is this?"

"She is my adopted daughter, I have no idea who her parents were," said Elieana but her nervous voice betrayed her.

"You had better have more answers, and with no delay, this girl's tattoo shows she is no commoner. She is of the line of Baltica."

Elieana fiddled with the alcove curtain, trying to think of an answer to satisfy him.

"If you do not tell me, I will have you arrested," said Darec and then he added so quietly Elieana had to strain to hear him, "Your daughter will be taken from you."

Elieana looked frantically at both men. Jorian, she knew. Darec, she did not know whether he threatened only to get answers or if he really meant what he said.

Jorian stepped forward, grasped Elieana's arm and led her to a chair. He pushed Elieana down into the chair then turned to Philen and nodded his head towards the door. Immediately Philen rose out of his chair, a look of empathy for Elieana on his face.

"Not a word, Philen," said Jorian.

Philen waved his hand in acknowledgement as he left the room and closed the door quietly behind him.

Jorian locked the door. The sound of the tumblers clicking into place sounded like a hammer hitting an anvil in Elieana's ears. Jorian looked directly at Elieana. With deadly firmness in his voice he ordered her to speak. "You will tell Darec all you know of this girl."

Elieana rubbed the back of her neck. Her hands fluttered nervously. "Please, I meant no harm. I found her during my journey from Belisle just before the outbreak of the war. She knows no other mother but me. She is my daughter because she has been with me for so long."

"What were you doing in Belisle?" said Darec.

"My husband was an Inlander, a Baltican, a healer in Belisle. We met before the war, when peace reigned between our two countries. Many years ago, my husband learned the Great Healing Knowledge while apprenticed to the chief healer of the Walled City. We met there while my father was Ambassador in Belisle. My parents lived in Belisle for many years until the order came from King Stephan that all foreigners must leave the city. I was already married. I chose to remain in Belisle with my husband.

"The people, including my husband's family and friends and our servants, ostracized us both because I was an Outsider. This wounded my husband very deeply. He stopped seeing his family and friends in support of me.

"My husband taught me the healing arts of the Great Knowledge. One night, while walking home from the market, murderers set upon him, robbed him, killed him." Her voice shook, and tears streamed down her cheeks.

"I knew then only a matter of time remained before I too would suffer the same fate. With the help of my most trusted servant, Valoren, the only one who remained with me, I planned my escape through the ancient tunnels under the city. No one knew when I left."

Her voice broke then, making it difficult for her to speak. Her hands shook as she poured herself a cup of water and drank slowly. She sat quietly, gazing at the wall as if past events played out in front of her. She shook her head sadly and started again, her voice barely a whisper. "I trusted Valoren with my life. Valoren grew up in my family's house." She sniffed and pulled out a handkerchief from her sleeve, wiped her face and blew her nose.

"Valoren took some of my belongings, and as we planned, I escaped the city. We met again outside the walls. " She choked as she recounted the ordeal. "The danger," she stopped and then continued in barely a whisper. "A few days before I left, the Queen and Princess Silanne vanished without a trace. King Stephan declared those responsible for her disappearance would be hung. He posted a reward for anyone supplying information of the Queen's whereabouts. People reported on their neighbors and family members. No one trusted anyone. Hatred and anger grew in the city and took on a life of its own."

Elieana licked her lips, sniffing and blinking back her tears. Jorian filled her cup again and they waited while she regained her composure. She drank slowly, not looking at the two men, purposely delaying the telling of her story.

"A few days into our journey, Valoren went hunting. I believe a Razora panther attacked him. He still lived when I found him but died from his wounds soon after.

"We were deep into the pass through the Razor Mountains. The pass is very treacherous. There are many places bandits hide and ambush travelers and at that time many soldiers patrolled the road. I took my chances on the bandit trail. Better to meet a bandit than be found by soldiers from Belisle. The bandit trail ran parallel to the roadway. It was far enough away that it could not be seen from the road. I saw many signs of their camps, their dead fires and trash left behind.

"At one point the trail ran very close to the road, but below it, at the base of a rocky outcropping. I came upon a carriage, damaged from running off the roadway above. It could not be seen from because of the thick shrubbery lining the roadway. It had not been there long, but I found no bodies, just the carcasses of two horses, still in harness and partially devoured.

"I was too afraid to stop in case whatever feasted on the horses would return. When I started to leave I heard a child crying from inside the carriage. I searched and found a secret compartment under a seat in the carriage and it was there I found the child, Silanne."

As Elieana spoke, the weight of many years of keeping her secret lifted from her shoulders. She had told no one this story, not even Nada. "I saw many tracks of animals and horses in the area, but I thought it too dangerous to follow them."

"Did you not..." Jorian started to ask a question but Elieana raised her hand to stop him. They sat and listened while she unburdened ten years from her conscience.

"The child's body was terribly bruised," whispered Elieana. She looked over at her daughter, fitfully sleeping. "When the carriage overturned, she must have been knocked unconscious for the compartment to remain undiscovered. Her hunger and thirst were fierce. Inside the compartment, I found other items; money and papers."

Elieana paused, she rose from her chair and poured another cup of water. She regarded both men carefully as if deciding whether she could trust them.

"The papers included Nada's pedigree, her position in line to the Baltican throne and hiding places of some of the family wealth."

Elieana's expression challenged Jorian and Darec, as if to say she would fight them for her right to keep Nada. "She is the daughter of King Stephan, the Princess Silanne."

Darec gripped the arms of the chair but he did not move. "It is good you have not revealed this to anyone else. You would have been dead long ago, as would she," said Darec.

"What do you mean?" said Elieana as she moved towards Nada in a protective manner.

Darec looked down at Nada. "The King of Baltica believed he had no natural living heir, so he adopted his nephew, Michael. With a kingdom within his grasp it would be difficult for Michael, the King's adopted son, to relinquish his position to the heir," said Darec. "Should she turn up," he added, his voice sounding ominous.

"We now believe there is an assassin amongst us. A poisoned sword injured Nada. Philen brought the sword to Jorian when he first found it. That is why I am here. It is fortunate for her you have knowledge of the poisons the assassins use. Why the assassin is here, I do not know. You can be certain, if he gains knowledge of Nada's pedigree, he will certainly use it to his advantage."

Elieana took a deep breath and then scowled at Darec as she blurted out, "How is it you, one of the Kings guards, know of the Healing Arts?"

He replied with equal scorn, "I am the grandson of Davien Faustus who was the Chief Physician in the capitol at that time. It is highly possible your husband and I met. My father trained me in the Healing Arts of the Great Knowledge before the revolt. No one in the Guild remained safe then. I remember that night well."

Elieana bowed her head slightly in acknowledgement of his rank in the Physician's Guild. "I have not met many members of the Guild. With its destruction nearly complete, I thought few were left to pass on their knowledge. How is it you came to be one of the King's guards in this city?"

"That is another story, for another time," said Darec. The look on his face stopped any further questions.

They were silent for a moment, gazing at each other, but each immersed in their own thoughts. A moan from Nada brought them back to the present. Elieana moved towards her daughter and touched her cheek with the back of her hand. Nada had a fever but Elieana knew that in a matter of time she would recover completely. Elieana now focused her attention solely with her daughter.

"When she is well, Elieana, I would speak with you again," said Darec realizing the futility of questioning her further.

Elieana waved her hand in acknowledgement, aware only of a slight clinking sound as the latch on the door fell home.

Chapter 3

Darec and Jorian stood in the stable, discussing, in low whispers, the events of the day and what the King's response would be when they told him the lost Baltican Princess resided in his city. His response would be severe when he learned she had been wounded. The poisoned sword caused them a great deal of worry. Neither man knew of anyone who had captured an assassin alive who would identify his Master, Girard. No one, other than Girard's own men, ever saw him in the flesh and lived.

A young soldier approached them, saluted by thumping his fist against his chest, then waited for Darec or Jorian to acknowledge him.

"What is it?" snarled Darec, not wanting to be interrupted.

"Devlyn, of the night watch, has not reported in," said the startled soldier.

"From what patrol?" said Darec, changing his tone from annoyance to concern.

"Along the shore to the fishing village and the seaward entrance to the castle. The watch saw him in the late evening, heading towards the village."

Darec and Jorian exchanged knowing glances. Jorian nodded to the soldier and then Darec and Jorian both walked away, leaving the soldier standing there with a bewildered look on his face.

"Soldier, report back to your Watch Commander. Thank you for your report," Darec called back over his shoulder.

Darec turned to Jorian, "The boy who brought you the sword, where can we find him?"

"Likely in Aldred's kitchen," replied Jorian.

"Well then, we will speak to him and have him show us exactly where he found it."

* * *

Philen slouched in a corner of the castle kitchen, a large bowl of purple beans on his lap. He didn't look much interested in shelling beans. He dropped more pods on the floor than into the bin beside him. Aldred scowled at him and slammed her spoon on her work counter with a loud crack.

"She's not dead, young man. Now get on with you, those have need to be done before the day is out."

When Philen saw Darec enter the kitchen he immediately focused all his attention on the beans, splitting them down the middle, sliding his thumb down the pod and popping the beans into the pot. Ensuring the husk went directly into the bin and not on the floor, where he had been carelessly dropping them.

Philen did not look up as Darec crossed the enormous kitchen. He fully expected a scolding from the man when he stopped in front of him. He couldn't help flinching slightly as he stared at the toes of Darec's boots.

Darec didn't speak to Philen but spoke over his shoulder to Aldred, where she stood near her massive stove, grumbling that they had no business in her kitchen.

"Aldred, I have need of Philen for the moment."

She began to say something then thought better of it when she saw the look on Darec's face. Philen watched out of the corner of his eye for her reaction. A look of disgust crossed her face and without a word she waved her large wooden spoon towards Philen and then towards the door, dismissing him.

Clearing his throat loudly as he left the kitchen Darec covered his mouth with his hand and turned his face so Aldred could not see the grin growing on his face. They had a common bond, the two of them, each putting on a tough face for the world.

Philen slid the pot of beans onto the counter next to Aldred and then followed Darec out of the kitchen at a discrete distance. As they passed through the door Philen spied Jorian, clutching a shovel and walking towards the castle gate. Before going through the gate Jorian stopped and waited for Darec and Philen to catch up.

"We want you to show us exactly where you found the sword," said Jorian, as they walked through the gate. Philen nodded then turned to his left and walked briskly towards the shore, in the direction of a large driftwood stump. When they arrived at the stump he pointed out the small hollow, on the seaward side of the stump, as the spot where he found the sword.

Jorian nodded grimly and started digging. After just two shovels full Jorian's shovel struck something. Whatever the shovel struck it yielded but not enough to let it go through. Jorian moved and started again and the same thing happened. He looked up at Darec and Philen, his expression bleak. "I think we've found our missing soldier," said Jorian.

Slowly they scraped away the sand and uncovered the man's body. Jorian removed the sand from the man's face, revealing an expression of surprise, frozen in rigor mortis. The gaping wound across his throat wore a crusted necklace of sickly green crystals.

"The sword's first victim", said Jorian as he wiped the sweat off his face with his sleeve.

"Don't let the sword take on a life of its own, Jorian, it is not the sword that is the killer but the killer himself. We will find the killer and he will pay."

"Philen," he said gruffly, "Can you find a dilhaa and cart and bring it here?"

Philen met Darec's gaze straight on and Darec noticed for the first time that the boy was probably fifteen or sixteen years, the age of his own son. He could see, in Philen's eyes, the deep mistrust. He knew he had been harsh to the boy, something which couldn't be helped with his nerves so raw and on edge. It had not been long since he had last seen his wife and children alive, before being killed by a roving band of mercenary soldiers. Darec realized he had no reason to be curt with Philen and clapped his hand on the boy's shoulder, attempting to lighten the mood. "See what you can find," and nodded his head towards the fishing village, sending Philen on his way.

Philen ran towards the village, to the home of Peter Bondar. He arrived at Peter's small shack, slightly out of breath. He wiped the sweat from his brow and ran his fingers through his hair, attempting to make himself presentable, then rapped loudly on the door. Peter called out through the thin walls of the shack and then opened the door. Peter was a somewhat plump, grey-haired man, friend to all he met. "Ah, Philen," said Peter and his face cracked into a huge grin. "I haven't seen you for some time, my boy. Where have you been hiding?"

"Oh, Aldred, she keeps me busy. I am sure I have shelled a whole field of beans by now and with my lessons, I have no time for anything else."

"Well, you are a boy no longer. You have grown taller than me. Soon you will stoop to come inside. Will you come in, have some refreshment?"

"I cannot, Peter, I am on an errand for Darec Redford."

Peter laughed, "You? The last I heard, you were running for your life from Darec. What has changed?"

"Not much, Peter. I am sure this is only for the moment. Darec will soon be back to his old self and again I will be running for my life." He laughed but the laughter did not show in his eyes and Peter could see something troubled him greatly.

"Can I borrow your cart and dilhaa for the day," Philip said.

"Well, little Dacy is in the paddock out back. She hasn't had much to do lately and will be happy to get out." Peter spoke fondly of his dilhaa, as if she were a member of his family. Dilhaas, smaller than a horse but strong and docile, were used for hauling lighter loads. Peter used his dilhaa for bringing his catch from his boat to the market but as Peter didn't fish every day his dilhaa stayed in the paddock with nothing to do but munch grass and sleep.

"Thank you, Peter. I will return her as soon as I can."

"No hurry, Philen, return it when you are finished. Next time maybe you will stay for a while."

"I will, Peter. Do you have a blanket or tarp in the wagon and can I take a jug of water as well? It's very hot out."

"There is a tarp under the wagon seat. Take what you need, Philen. I have a stone bottle you can use, just filled at the well." Peter walked back into his house to fetch the bottle then watched as Philen harnessed the dilhaa to the cart. Philen tightened the harness with a rough hand, causing the dilhaa to bleat and squirm. He slapped the creature hard on the withers to make it stop. Peter had never seen Philen be cruel to an animal before. He shook his head sadly, thinking it must be something very serious to make Philen act this way.

When Philen had climbed up into the seat, Peter handed him the stone bottle, then squeezed his arm gently. "Come back later, Philen, I think there is much for us to talk about."

Philen looked grimly at Peter and only nodded in response, then shook the reins and turned the dilhaa to where Darec and Jorian waited for him.

Peter watched Philen drive the cart down the road, massaging the back of his neck, as he always did, when something disturbed him.

Once out on the road, Philen cracked the long whip he found in the cart over the dilhaa's back. Alarmed by the loud noise the dilhaa let out a bleat of surprise and broke into a run, jerking the cart forward. Almost losing his perch on the seat from the sudden forward jolt, Philen cracked the whip again, this time in anger. He felt miserable. Philen tried to think of other things as the cart bumped over the roadway. He watched the dilhaa's head bobbing as it plodded along and guiltily realized that the dilhaa was doing its best to pull the cart along the rocky roadway. Philen wished he had never risen from his bed that morning. So much misery for one day.

Philen descended further into the blackness of his mood as he absentmindedly drove the cart towards its grisly cargo. His worry for Nada grew in his heart, as well as anger at the death of Devlyn, the guardsman. Two short days before, Philen and Devlyn wrestled each other over a pan full of fruit. Now, Devlyn, only three years older than Philen, lay unceremoniously dumped in a hole, his throat slit ear to ear.

A loud shout shook Philen back to the present. He looked back over his shoulder to see Darec waving at him from the beach. Completely engrossed in his miserable thoughts he had passed the spot where Jorian and Darec waited. He turned the cart around and flicked the whip, this time being careful, so it got the dilhaa's attention and did not startle it.

The dilhaa's grunts, as it pulled the cart across the sand, sounded so comical that for just a second Philen felt a gurgle of laughter deep down in his throat. The feeling disappeared just as quickly when he looked towards the two men standing by the body they had just exhumed.

Darec's face glowed red from exertion. He mopped it with a large kerchief all the while grumbling that Philen had taken too long. Philen decided to ignore Darec's irritable remarks. He reached down under the seat for the stone bottle Peter had given him. "I brought you a jug of water, thought you might be a bit thirsty," said Philen, with a cheerfulness he didn't feel, as he passed the bottle to Darec.

Darec stuffed the kerchief back in his pocket, a look of surprise flickering across his face, then he hid it with the stern look he usually wore. "Thank you, Philen," said Darec as he reached out and took the proffered bottle. He sloshed some of the water over his face, then took a long drink. Wiping his mouth with his sleeve he passed the jug to Jorian, who had just finished filling in the hole.

Jorian jammed the shovel into the sand, drank from the jug then poured the rest over his head. He shook his head back and forth like a dog, spraying droplets of water in every direction. "That's fine, Philen, thank you for bringing the cart and water," said Jorian. "I am about dried up and ready to blow away with this heat."

They rested for a moment longer, then Darec patted Jorian on the shoulder. "Come Jorian, let's get our friend into the cart and back to the castle. We'll have to clean him ourselves to make sure none of the poison remains."

Jorian passed the bottle back to Philen and then Darec and Jorian gently lifted the dead man's body into the cart, covered it with the tarp and carefully tucked it around the body. To Philen it seemed they took extra care so as not to waken him. He realized, while watching them, this was very difficult for them both. Even though the young guardsman had been with the garrison for a short while they had bonded, like a family. This day, promising to be a glorious one for all of them, turned out to be a black one indeed.

Darec tucked the empty scabbard they found in the hole under the tarp beside the body then slowly they all rode back to the castle. Jorian and Darec sat up front on the seat; Philen sat at the back with his legs dangling down over the edge staring trancelike at the tracks the cart left in the sand and absentmindedly listened to the dilhaa working hard, snuffling and grunting when the cartwheels bogged down.

Finally, taking pity on the poor little beast, Philen jumped down and walked along behind, pushing the cart when the wheels got stuck. When they reached the road, Philen hopped up on the cart again. Once again on the hard-packed roadway travel became easier. The dilhaa stopped panting and grunting. Its feet slapped rhythmically on the roadway, in time to the distant sound of the surf as the tide slowly came in.

No one spoke. Deep in thought Philen reviewed the events of the day as he dumped the sand out of his shoes. Why bury a sword there? Why kill the guardsman? It seemed like it might have been an accident that Devlyn met his death. There did not seem to be any reason for the guardsman to die. Philen decided, in his own mind, the guardsman stumbled onto the person who had the sword and was killed for it. He shivered with the thought that someone in the city killed in fear of discovery? What kind of a person would do that? More importantly, who was he?

The cart jerked over a bump, knocking Philen sideways onto the cadaver's stiff legs and causing him to drop his shoe. He pushed himself away, feeling slightly sick from touching the stiff, cold corpse. The tang of bile stung the back of his throat. He had never been this close to a dead man. Suddenly, he realized he had to get off the cart or lose what little respect he had gained in the men's eyes.

Stumbling slightly as he jumped down he leaned forward with his hands on his knees and his head down, gulping in deep breaths of air. When the sick feeling passed, he retrieved his shoe then glanced up to see the cart had already passed through the castle gate. Philen ran to catch up but slowed to a walk once he entered the dark coolness of the passage through the thick castle walls.

As soon as he walked into the passageway he felt someone's eyes upon him. He couldn't see, after being in the bright sunlight, but he could make out the shape of someone standing under the arch, his back pushed tightly against the wall. Philen couldn't make out the person's face but he could smell him. For sure one of the gong farmers stood concealed in the shadows. They never strayed far from their part of the village, inside the old walled town, mainly because others could not stand the smell of them. Odd, Philen thought, it seems he is hiding. He took a quick look again at the man but as he could not make out his face and thinking it unimportant, he ran to catch up with the cart.

* * *

Darcc drove the cart through the village, bumping over the cobbles, and then turned into a narrow street, the street of the undertakers. Gloom settled down over them, causing a shiver of dread to run up Philen's spine. The narrow lanes and the houses overhanging the street did not allow the sun to penetrate to the street below.

At the end of the street they stopped beside a shabby and unkempt, rough-built house. The wooden sign, hanging crookedly above the door, identified the establishment as 'J.S. Black, Mortician and Cabinet Maker.' Jorian backed the cart up in front of a smaller building beside it then climbed down off the cart seat. Before they had an opportunity to knock on the door a thin, balding man opened it; he gazed over their heads at the back of the cart and nodded. He smiled, toothily and bade them enter.

"Philen, stay with the cart," said Jorian, as he entered the building.

With a sigh, Philen leaned against the wall, preferring a huge pot of beans to shell at this very moment. He reached over and patted the dilhaa then loosened the harness. The dilhaa snuffled and nudged him with its nose so Philen led it over to a trough nearby. An oily slick covered the murky water in the trough but the dilhaa dipped its face down and started sucking large gulps without a second thought.

A hound's angry barking drew Philen's attention from watching the dilhaa slake its thirst to the narrow alley at the back of the building. When he reached the rear corner of the building, he saw a ragged man with long straggly hair running in the opposite direction. No breeze moved the air in the alley and the pungent smell of the man hung thickly in the air, causing Philen to pinch his nostrils shut. He only caught a glimpse of the man's face, gaunt with a prominent nose. Philen shrugged. "Probably looking to rob the corpse," he said to himself and he walked back to the front of the building, thinking nothing more about the man running away.

Philen returned to find the dilhaa with its head hanging down, sleeping a well-earned rest after its struggles on the beach. With nothing else to do Philen sat down on the porch of the house to wait for Darec and Jorian.

After what seemed like hours, Darec and Jorian exited the house. Darec grumbled loudly. "It is highway robbery what he is charging us." He held up his money pouch and shook its contents with a disgusted look on his face then shoved it inside his jerkin.

Jorian slapped his friend on the shoulder to console him then opened the double doors of the smaller building, revealing a large stone slab, a pump and metal basins for water and a brazier with a bucket of charcoal beside it.

Startled, Philen realized that Darec and Jorian meant it when they said they would clean the body themselves. Apprehensively he watched them back the cart as far into the building as they could and then they lifted the body onto the slab.

Once they emptied the cart they pulled it out and closed and bolted one of the doors then Darec took his leave to retrieve his box of powders to cleanse the poison from the man's body.

Jorian watched Darec walk down the street then turned to Philen, "I won't be long, Philen. Under no circumstances are you to leave the shed."

Philen's eyes widened in shock. "Where are you going?" he squeaked, revealing his panic.

"I must go to the barracks and get clothing for Devlyn, so we can return him to his family," he replied without reacting to Philen's discomfort.

"But Darec can go, he can get those things," said Philen. His anxiousness caused his face to turn pale and sweaty

"No, Philen, he must get his medicine box. It will take us longer to get this dreaded job done if only one of us gathers up all we require. I'll not be gone long. Latch the door, let no one in," said Jorian, then he walked away down the gloomy street.

Philen watched him until he turned the corner, hoping Jorian only teased. When Jorian didn't reappear, Philen looked around, wondering what to do. Finally, he tentatively walked to the shed and entered, staying as far as he could from the dead man. To keep the dark gloom of the windowless building at bay Philen found a candle and lit it before he closed and bolted the door. He pulled a stool over to the wall and sat in the shadows waiting for Jorian and Darec to return. The eeriness of sitting in semi-darkness with the body of the guardsman laid out so still and the flickering candlelight dancing on the walls unnerved Philen, as if the man's presence remained.

After a long while of staring at the man under his shroud Philen reached over and touched his startlingly cold hand. At the same moment, a crash sounded outside causing the dilhaa to bray loudly.

Philen jumped off the stool, nearly braining himself on one of the roof supports. His heart pounded in his chest. Holding his breath while rubbing his head he listened for any more movement outside. "It must have been a scavenger," he whispered to himself, which he desperately wanted to believe. He fought down images of someone breaking down the door and slitting his throat as they did to the guard. Tense and alert, he stood listening for any further sounds. After a long wait and no other sounds of movement outside he regained his perch on the stool.

The unbearably long wait ended with the return of Jorian first and Darec arriving shortly afterwards. Philen had dozed off and when Jorian rapped lightly on the door he leapt off the stool, crouched and ready for attack.

"Philen, open the door," said Jorian as he rapped again loudly.

Recognizing Jorian's voice Philen rubbed his face vigorously. When he had regained his composure he unlatched the door, pulling it wide open. He could have hugged Jorian and stepped aside so the men could enter the room. Jorian carried a sack which he hung from a peg on the wall.

"Philen, will you pump water into one of the basins?" said Jorian.

Darec lit the brazier and then from the sack he withdrew a small, intricately decorated, metal box. A carved snake wound around a staff on the lid, its ruby eyes glowing in the firelight seemed alive, as if they were blinking. Darec took out a small metal cup from a pouch, a piece of metal and a vial of white powder. Philen watched with interest as Darec proceeded to cleanse the green crystals from the wound on the dead man's neck and stood in awe as he watched the crystals change from the ugly green to an even uglier yellow then slowly fade, leaving a powdery, pure-white substance in the bottom of the cup.

Darec cleansed the wound three times to ensure no poisonous residue remained. Then, using a small needle and fine thread, he stitched the wound closed. Philen respected Darec for the care he took in tending to the dead guardsman. When Darec had finished stitching the wound it showed only as a thin line across the man's neck. If they positioned his head slightly downwards no one could see it.

They cut off the soiled clothes and stuffed them in the sack Jorian brought with him. They cleaned the dirt and dust off the body, dressed him in clean clothes and combed his hair. The soldier looked as if he had just fallen asleep.

Darec meticulously cleaned his tools and placed them back in the box. Philen stuffed the used tarp into the sack with the clothes for burning later. When they finally reopened the doors of the shed, twilight had settled on the street like a blanket. The murkiness closed in on them and no light escaped the shuttered lower windows of the nearby houses.

Jorian reversed the cart as far inside the building as he could, to load the body, then they covered it with a clean blanket.

Darec emptied the brazier into a slop heap behind the building and threw water on the coals, causing them to hiss and smoke. Returning to the cart Darec gave Philen's shoulder a slight squeeze. "Thank you, Philen, you have done well, to stay here alone with the body."

Philen nodded, but did not smile at the compliment. To do so, now, seemed disrespectful. However, the compliment, coming from Darec, meant much.

"Come, young man, we will take our friend home then you may take a much-needed rest."

"But Aldred," replied Philen, suddenly feeling guilty for not finishing his work. "She will want the rest of the beans shelled."

"I think your bean shelling days are over. You have proven yourself today. Tomorrow you will come and train as my aide."

Philen looked at Darec in disbelief.

"I do not jest. I have misjudged you. You deserve the opportunity and will make your family proud. Come, your day is almost done, and I will expect you at my quarters when the sun rises."

Philen hitched the dilhaa to the cart, Darec's words making it much easier. None of them rode this time. Although weary from their toil and the emotion they all felt, the guardsman should ride in the cart alone. Their most difficult task of the day, to take him home to his waiting family. The three men walked slowly at the front of the cart, guiding the dilhaa through the village streets, each man alone with his thoughts of that long and troubling day.

Chapter 4

Nada slowly regained consciousness. She tried to wet her cracked lips with her tongue, but it seemed too big for her mouth. Nausea churned her stomach. Her foot throbbed. She winced in pain as she pulled her foot up. Lightly running her fingers along the bottom of her foot she felt the heat emanating from her skin. It felt swollen and hot to touch.

Recollection crept like a thief into her mind. She remembered the children in the courtyard screaming at her, but why? Feeling very alone she reached over and pulled aside the curtain surrounding her bed. The flicker of a single candle lit the desk where Elieana slept in a chair, her head back, snoring softly.

"Wa ... water please, Elieana," her voice came out in a croak.

Elieana lifted her head and massaged the kink out of her neck. She rubbed her eyes and a look of amazement spread across her face. "You're awake. Oh, Nada, I feared the worst, you have been asleep for so long."

"How long have I been asleep?" Nada swallowed, trying to dampen her throat.

"Since you injured your foot. You had such a fever. You rambled, Nada. So many strange things you said. I haven't left your side."

Elieana poured a cup of water and hurried to Nada's bed. When Nada finished, Elieana scooped her up into her arms. She hugged the girl tightly while silent tears ran down her cheeks. "I thought I would lose you. Oh, Nada, I love you so."

Nada gently pushed her away then reached up to wipe the tears from Elieana's face. "You didn't need to worry, Elieana. I never will leave you. I love you too much."

Elieana hugged her again, avoiding her eyes, then got up from the bed. "Are you hungry? Aldred will be overjoyed when she hears you are awake." Elieana knew she was chattering but for some reason she had to keep talking, if not she may break down from the anxiety and worry she felt since Nada slashed her foot and the appearance of Darec at their door.

"Thank you. Some bread please, Elieana."

Elieana refilled the cup and passed it to Nada watching as she drank her fill. Nada's eyes, huge in the dim light, shone with love for her mother. Fear tightened Elieana's throat, knowing the danger existing around them. I must get her away from here before others discover who she is, thought Elieana.

A plan materialized in Elieana's mind; a small sack of food from the kitchen; with the concealment of the night they could leave the castle; take one of the small boats from the fishing village. Guiltily she convinced herself she would not be stealing the boat when the taking was for personal safety.

The sea dragons did not hunt at night, there should be no danger and they could stay close to shore. They could travel down the coastline until they came to another village. She could always find work as a healer. When Nada recovered fully they could travel farther away from Pelagos and Baltica, perhaps to the Dragon Islands. Her plan anchored her, replacing her fear for Nada's safety.

Nada watched Elieana as she rummaged through drawers, gathering clothes and her medicines. Elieana's odd behaviour worried Nada but she didn't have the strength to question her. She pulled the bedclothes up under her chin then noticed a strange mark on the palm of her right hand. "I wonder how I got that mark?" she whispered groggily, trying to remember what happened after she slashed her foot, but it took too much energy to think so she turned her head towards the wall and closed her eyes.

"I'll return soon, Nada. Don't get out of bed," said Elieana. She paused for a moment before leaving, "Will you be all right while I go to the kitchen?"

"I will but please hurry back," said Nada without opening her eyes. She didn't want to be alone; she felt very small, very frightened and her foot throbbed with pain that traveled up her leg. Elieana patted Nada's back gently then left the room, locking the door behind her.

When Elieana reached the courtyard she glanced up, to ensure no guards stood on the wall. She slipped into the wall's heavy shadow, the silence of the night enfolding her as she crept along. The sliver of the moon and tiny stars glittering in the deep velvety blackness of the sky did little to light her way.

As she crept along, she told herself over and over, like a mantra, they would be safe if they traveled close to shore. There were places where they could cross to the islands without going into deep water. How else were fishermen bringing in their catch without fear of the sea dragons?

When Elieana reached the kitchen she gently pushed the door open and peeked in. Warm air scented with the smell of bread and spices wafted through the opening. Due to the time of night none of the cooks remained, all having sought out their tiny pallets to rest before the bustle of the new day. Elieana quietly slipped inside, closing the door without a sound.

* * *

Aldred sat dozing in her chair, soaking up the last warmth from the fading fire in the huge kitchen hearth. The familiar creak of the door as it opened behind her, alerted her to someone entering the kitchen.

Whoever crept through the kitchen muttered quietly and moved about with stealth. They could not know they were overheard as Aldred's huge chair sat in the shadows and concealed her presence. Aldred listened intently and recognized Elieana's voice. She started to rise but then stopped herself. Although Aldred could not make out what Elieana said, she assumed it had to do with Nada. It had worried Aldred from the start, not just Nada's injury but how Elieana had become more and more agitated.

Aldred peered around the edge of her armchair and watched as Elieana filled a small sack with bread, vegetables and dried meat. She stuffed the sack inside her jerkin and stealthily left the kitchen. Aldred knew Elieana's headstrong and determined character. When she put her mind to something no one could do or say anything to stop her. She waited a short while to be sure Elieana would not return then she hefted herself out of the chair. "Darec will know what to do about Elieana's fears," she said under her breath. Aldred knew everything that went on in the castle. The death of the young guardsman and Nada's injury was common knowledge. The cooks' gossip flew around the kitchen, as they tried to put the pieces together of every event that took place. Aldred found it best just to listen and gather the information until a picture formed in her mind.

Only a few people, including Aldred, knew of the poisoned sword and how the guard met his untimely death. It was not difficult to guess that Elieana was leaving because of Nada's injury but why, with such secrecy. When she reached the officer's quarters she asked the soldier standing guard to summon Darec. Hearing the menacing tone in her voice he promptly left her standing in the shadows to seek Darec out.

Darec opened the door of the barracks and looked at Aldred quizzically. She shrugged at him, a lopsided smile flitting across her face, "A lady of the night I'm not."

"Aldred, I would rather meet you than any lady of the night," said Darec.

Aldred chuckled softly then pulled Darec away from the door. An expression of surprise flashed across his face as she did so and caused a bubble of laughter to ripple through her chest. "Elieana came to the kitchen a short while ago, very agitated and talking to herself. She filled a sack with food then left. I think she is planning to leave and take Nada away with her."

"I will take care of this. You go back to your fire, Aldred," said Darec.

Aldred didn't need any more information. She knew Darec would set things right and trusted him do so. With a nimbleness on her feet that amazed Darec, Aldred strode down the passageway back to the kitchen and the warmth of her hearth. Darec hurried off in the opposite direction, towards Elieana's chamber, keeping to the shadows so as not to be seen.

Chapter 5

When Elieana returned to her chamber it didn't take long for her to convince Nada they must leave. She helped Nada bundle into warm clothes, a jerkin and leather pants. Elieana lifted Nada off the bed and carried her to the door. She took one last look around at all her possessions, what remained of her previous life. She sighed sadly then opened the door to find Darec about to knock.

"Where are you going, Elieana?"

"I ... I'm ..."

"Elieana, she's ill. She can't travel and there are questions that need to be answered."

"Darec, please, let us go."

"No, you go back inside, we must talk," said Darec as he gently pushed her back inside the room.

Elieana's shoulders slumped, realizing Darec knew too much. Leaving was pointless. She held tightly onto Nada, as if the tighter she held on, the less chance something could hurt her or take her away.

"Elieana," Nada struggled in her arms, "You're crushing me."

Elieana loosened her grip and Darec took Nada from her. The girl reached up and put her arms around Darec's neck which caused him to immediately turn a dark shade of red.

Nodding towards the open doorway Darec followed Elieana back into the room. She flopped into a large chair, dropped the sack on the floor, then leaned forward with her head in her hands.

Darec carried Nada to her cot; he covered her with a thick quilt then reached over and very gently smoothed her hair off her face. She still had the rounded forehead of a much younger girl. She did not look like the young woman she was. What a beautiful girl, he thought, very much like my Karina. Nada smiled drowsily back at him then closed her eyes and swiftly dropped off to sleep.

Quietly Darec drew the curtain across the alcove then sat down across from Elieana. He didn't say a word to her, he just sat and waited until she lifted her head and looked at him. Stress showed visibly on her face. Tiny lines on her brow seemed deeper than he remembered from their first meeting.

They sat quietly for some time until Elieana spoke, "Why did you stop me?"

Smiling grimly, Darec replied, "I would rather stop you than have to pursue you."

"Who would have known or cared until we were long gone?"

"As one of the King's soldiers I would be obligated to pursue you. I care that Nada would be at risk. Many in the castle would notice you were gone; it would not have been long before we, of the guard, also noticed. I also would not like to see you put in the dungeons."

"Darec, they will put me there. I have King Stephan's daughter. They will speculate I initiated the disappearance of the Queen and Princess after the death of my husband. There is no hope for me."

"You must also have the papers to prove who Nada is. How else would you have them unless you had found her, as you have said? If we go back to the site of the wrecked carriage perhaps there is a clue to how the accident happened. Perhaps there is a village nearby in which someone might recall the accident or the bodies. You also owe it to Nada. She is King Stephan's rightful heir. She will lose her inheritance if he claims Michael before the wedding."

"Perhaps we will find it," said Elieana. "Perhaps someone will remember the crash, but I expect no clues remain at the site. The danger in taking the packet with me was too great so I buried it in oilcloth at the foot of a tree nearby the wreck. The packet may still be intact, but likely not."

"Well then, we will go find it and if it is still there, bring the packet back and present it to the King. Perhaps there may be something or someone who will lead us to the truth of what happened that day. I am sure Aldred will be more than happy to take care of Nada while we are gone."

Hopelessly Elieana nodded, "I will show you where it is and enjoy this short period of freedom."

"Get some rest, Elieana. We will depart before first light. Pack lightly but bring warm clothes."

Elieana let Darec out and bolted the door, then she lay down on her bed fully clothed. She quickly fell into a deep sleep and dreamt strange and frightening dreams of swirling fog, large and frightening creatures, darkness and a terrible sense of loss.

* * *

Darec returned to the barracks to speak to Jorian. They agreed that Jorian would arrange an audience with King Albryk the following day and inform him of Nada's presence and her injury. Jorian agreed to wait until morning before he spoke to the King so that Darec and Elieana would be able to reach the outer gates of Pelagos in the event the King called for Darec to return.

Darec knew the best place for Nada to recover was in familiar surroundings and with Elieana, the only person she had relied on for most of her young life. The chamber they shared, Darec thought, was the safest place for her as no one knew her other than as Nada, the healer's daughter. He also knew that although it may be the safest place, the King would not allow her to remain there. It was best that Elieana did not know that Nada would be moved to the castle. Darec knew he would not be able to get Elieana to leave if Nada was taken to the King before they left Pelagos. He also believed Elieana would not trust him if she knew he had arranged for Nada to be moved before they left.

Jorian and Darec both agreed that Aldred should care for Nada. Darec trusted Aldred without reservation and knew she would guard Nada with her life until Jorian came to remove her to the castle. Darec sought out Aldred and found her still sitting in her chair, the fire grown cold. She sat, waiting for him, as if she expected him to return, but Darec knew that the slightest noise in Aldred's kitchen would alert her to his presence. If she had been sleeping she would not have told him and he wondered then, where did she sleep.

Immediately after Darec left the kitchen Aldred went about completing the tasks she normally did in the early morning before her assistants came to start the bread. She lit the ovens to warm them and filled the kettles with water to simmer on the stove top. Aldred rekindled the fire in the hearth and then took a large blanket from a chest near her chair, wrapped it around her shoulders and set off to Elieana's chamber.

Chapter 6

Elieana awoke abruptly to a scratching sound at the door. She stumbled as she got off her bed. Not quite awake, she rubbed her eyes, furiously. She opened the door a crack to reveal Aldred standing there wrapped in a large wool blanket.

"Don't worry about Nada," said Aldred, as she pushed herself into the room. "I'll take good care of her and when I have to be in the kitchen I will send Elise to sit with her." She patted Elieana on the shoulder as she moved over to a chair big enough to hold her bulk. Aldred had a presence, not just because of her size but her capability and kindness. Any problem or difficult situation diminished in size when Aldred came to the rescue.

Elieana watched as Aldred settled herself down in the chair, wrapping herself snugly in the blanket then waving her hand in dismissal. "Go with Darec, Elieana. You have a long way to travel, in a very short time."

The next moment Darec arrived. Elieana wondered how much he had told Aldred. He shrugged his shoulders as if he knew her thoughts and his mouth twitched in something like a grin as he glanced over at Aldred ensconced in the chair. He reached down and picked up the bag of food Elieana left on the floor and tucked the bag into his jerkin.

Darec took a leather jerkin from a peg by the door along with a heavy woolen coat and passed them to Elieana. Elieana donned the coat and jerkin. She took a pair of leather gauntlets and a scarf from a drawer, wrapped the scarf around her neck and pulled on the gauntlets. She went to Nada's little alcove and gently kissed her forehead, being careful not to waken her. She gazed lovingly at her daughter who had been so much a part of her life. She quickly wiped away a tear that escaped down her cheek then walked out the door without looking back.

Instead of descending to the courtyard Darec led Elieana up the winding stairway from her chamber. He stopped at a small balcony, overlooking the oily black sea below. The waning moon's weak glow barely left a glimmer on the water. Darec pressed a stone block at the base of the wall and a hidden door popped open a crack. He opened it further to reveal a very narrow stairway winding down and disappearing into pitch-blackness.

Elieana clenched her fists tightly. It seemed like the entrance to the underworld and her feet felt as if they were frozen to the floor of the passageway.

"There is a rope along the wall, take hold and go to the bottom," said Darec as he held the door for her.

Elieana took a deep breath to calm herself and to remove her feelings of foreboding then grasped the rope. The door shut with a muffled thud and they were plunged into darkness. Somewhat startled by the sudden inability to see she held on with both hands as if the rope were a lifeline.

Darec whispered in her ear, "Let me pass by you so I can open the door at the bottom." He squeezed past her and as he passed she could smell his scent, a leather and wood smoke smell which immediately comforted her. Darec proceeded to the bottom of the stairwell and Elieana could hear Darec searching for the latch to open the next door, then the scraping of rock on rock as he pushed it open. The smell of the sea wafted in, a salt tang on the cool breeze. The open doorway below gave Elieana a focal point to move towards. When she reached the bottom she gratefully stepped through the opening, just large enough for Darec to squeeze through.

A narrow path led down onto a rocky beach and she could see that at high tide it would be completely covered by water. An outcropping of rock forming part of the foundation of the castle further obscured the door. Unless someone approached the castle from the sea, at low tide, the pathway and beach would be completely obscured.

Two horses tethered nearby whickered softly as they approached. They tied their belongings behind the saddles then walked the horses far out on the sand, so their hoof prints would be washed away with the incoming tide. They skirted the fishing village and accessed a narrow trail through some boggy areas and scrub brush.

"Darec, where are you going?" said Elieana when she could finally ride abreast of him.

"We will take a roundabout way to get to the gate. There are strange goings on at the castle. It may have to do with the wedding, but I do not know, yet. I have arranged for the watchman to open a gate in the outer wall, so we must hurry before his watch is ended."

They rode through forest bordering flat pasture lands, keeping close to the river where the trees grew thick and the mist, rising from the river bottom, concealed them as they passed. Sometime later the high wall at the north end of the peninsula loomed up in front of them, darker than the sky above. Darec stopped and whistled softly, a sound almost like a night lark. Immediately Elieana saw a flicker of light, as if someone lit a pipe. Darec waved his hand for Elieana to follow him and they proceeded towards the wall. They had not gone very far when a man seemed to materialize in front of them. He held a dark cloak wrapped tightly about his body. He whispered something then Darec dismounted, motioning for Elieana to do the same.

They led their horses, single file until Elieana heard the metallic scrape of a latch bolt lifting and a cough from the watchman as he tried to obscure the noise. The heavy door swung open silently. They led the horses into a wide tunnel where sand covered the floor, muffling the sound of the horse's hooves as they passed through. When they reached the far end the watchman opened the last door and they exited out into the open country on the south side of the wall. Elieana heard the latch bolt pushed home with a clunk. The sound of finality.

It felt very strange being out in the countryside. Elieana had not been outside of the wall since arriving at the castle a few years before. She felt as if a safety net had been pulled out from under her, sweeping away any security she had gained. Elieana felt very alone and very vulnerable.

They again mounted their horses and traveled south along the Kofathi River until it split into the River Noor and the Samos River which flowed back through the valley towards the sea. Darec led Elieana across the Samos River at a low spot. Even though the Samos River was wide and rocky, it still ran swiftly, making the crossing treacherous.

Upon reaching the opposite bank they followed the river southwest towards Baltica and the city of Belisle. They traveled along the riverbank until they came upon a game trail leading deep into the forest. Both sides of the trail were thick with an overgrowth of tall Rough Bark and aromatic Ginka trees; below, thick shrubbery, vines and brambles caught at their clothing as they passed.

Remembering Valoren, Elieana clutched the reins tightly. She didn't speak, to do so seemed like a disruption of the forest's natural order. No birds sang, no insects or reptiles chirped as they passed. Neither of them spoke, each absorbed with their own thoughts until Elieana broke the silence. "Do you think these 'goings on' you spoke of are related to Nada's injury?" said Elieana.

It took Darec some time to answer. "Yes, but she was not meant to be a victim. I believe someone botched his job, which is why she got hurt. I did not tell you before because I did not know how much I should tell you. You are deeply involved; therefore, you must know the truth. A young guardsman died that night. We found him buried in the same spot where Nada slashed her foot."

Elieana stopped her horse, her stomach clenched with anxiety. "You mean below where she sat that morning?" she asked quietly.

Darec stopped and took hold of the reins of her mount. Her face contorted, turned red, then she burst into tears. Her body shook with emotion as she sobbed. This took Darec by surprise. He believed from the first moment he met her she had a great deal of strength. This display of emotion did not fit with his opinion of her. He didn't know what to do and sat there watching her, stunned into silence. Tears ran freely down Elieana's red and swollen face. Darec didn't know whether he should turn away or continue watching her. Feeling totally helpless he reached into his pocket, pulled out a yellow square of fabric and pushed it into her hand. "Take it, to wipe your tears away," he said somewhat more gruffly than he had intended.

She looked at him with huge, sad eyes. Her lips quivered as if she may start crying again. He reached over and took the square from her and gently wiped her face. She took it from him then and turned away. She wiped her face and blew her nose then sheepishly handed the square back to him. He took it back and stuffed it into the pouch hanging on the side of his saddle.

"We will find a solution to this problem," said Darec, attempting to comfort her. "We will find the packet where you buried it. Surely, we can convince the King your intentions were honorable. You know, though, this will change matters regarding the wedding. It is imperative we have the packet before the wedding takes place because Nada will be the next in line for the Baltican throne, not Michael as King Stephan's adopted son."

Elieana nodded and sniffed as she tried to regain her composure.

"I took her with me because she was alone and scared and hungry. The danger at that time, the unrest..." her voice trailed off.

"It is only recently travel has become possible between the cities. But Darec, I love her as my own. I knew someday I would have to return her to her family, but I have been so afraid to lose her, you see, I have no one else."

"Elieana, you can never know how much I understand."

Her eyes looked so tragic. He suddenly felt that he should hold her in his arms. Not wanting to show a softer side he abruptly straightened up in the saddle, the hard outer-shell Darec portrayed for all to see settling firmly back on his shoulders. "We must travel," he said as he passed the reins back to her. He gave his mount a nudge with his heels and jogged ahead.

Elieana didn't follow right away. She watched him go for just a moment before she followed at a slower pace. Confused by his abruptness and embarrassed by her emotional outburst, she fell back further and further so she would not have to make conversation and he could not see the emotion remaining on her face.

The towering trees overshadowed the trail but occasional breaks in the thickness of the overgrowth revealed the sun high in the sky. Elieana felt the quiet of the forest unnerving, as if nothing lived here. She lost sight of Darec as he rounded a bend in the trail and nudged her horse with her heels to get it to move faster. When she rounded the bend, she saw Darec stopped ahead in a tiny clearing, surrounded by a group of heavily armed men.

Without further thought Elieana slipped the sword from the scabbard beside her saddle. She whipped her mount to run faster and rushed towards the group of men. They broke the circle around Darec when they saw Elieana rushing towards them, their mounts pawing the ground in agitation. Darec shouted and threw up his arms for Elieana to stop. As she came abreast of him he reached out and grabbed the reins of her mount. The horse's head pulled back, but the momentum of its body still moved forward. Elieana lost her grip on the sword and it flew out of her hand, landing harmlessly in the dirt. Elieana, not so lucky, fell off, landing heavily on her side.

Darec jumped down, ran to Elieana and helped her to sit up as he dusted the dirt and debris from her clothing.

Elieana babbled at him, stunned from the fall, "Why did you stop me? Who are those men? What were they doing?"

"Elieana, I'm sorry. I had some of my men leave the castle by different routes. We intended to meet further down the trail but a Razora panther attacked them. They came to warn us."

"What attacked them?" she asked as she pushed herself up off the ground, rubbing her bruised shoulder.

"A Razora panther," replied one of the guardsmen to her left.

Someone came from behind her, reached down and gave her his hand to pull her up off the ground. When she looked up, Philen stood beside her, a very large grin on his face.

"Hello, Elieana, how is Nada?"

"Recovering, Philen, what are you doing here?" Confused she looked from Philen to Darec.

Darec shrugged, "He did well in helping us uncover the sword Nada slashed her foot on. He has been promoted."

Elieana nodded as she straightened her clothing and then she again climbed back on her horse. As she adjusted herself in the saddle the men discreetly looked away, giving her the opportunity to regain her dignity. When she was seated in her saddle Elieana looked up at the tiny patch of sky above and as if on cue her stomach grumbled. Remembering she had not eaten since the night before she reached down into her pouch to get out some of the food she had brought along. Darec gripped her arm and stopped her. Startled, she jerked her hand back and a stab of fear ran through her body as she realized they could be in grave danger.

All the men watched Darec, waiting for him to make the decision to move out. He listened intently for a moment more and then waved his arm in a forward motion without saying a word. They proceeded swiftly along the path, which only allowed them to ride single file and when the path widened the faster the men rode.

A tight band of tension grew across Elieana's chest as she wondered what it was that made them move so hurriedly. Surely, they had dispatched the panther. She knew they did not hunt in packs; there should be no more danger. The faster the animals moved; the harder Elieana had to concentrate on staying in the saddle; the less she could worry about any animal attacking them.

They finally turned onto a wider trail which steadily climbed higher and higher into the mountains. Elieana thought they must be getting close to where she had found the carriage. Although she didn't recognize any landmarks, she knew they were heading in the general direction of the city of Belisle.

It amazed Elieana that Darec found the trail so easily but on second thought he probably knew about it. He seemed to have a general idea of where to find the wreck when she initially told him about it.

After traveling a fair distance from where they had joined the rest of Darec's men, they slowed the tired horses to a walk. Darec and Elieana had been riding most of the night and a good portion of the day. Elieana felt her tiredness seeping into her bones. They turned off the trail, heading in a westerly direction until they came to a small meadow marked by a large outcropping of rocks where Darec announced they would stop for the night. A spring nearby created a pool of water surrounded by large ferns and plants with huge creamy colored flowers, sweetly scenting the air.

Elieana dismounted. Her leg muscles quivered from riding for so long and her side ached from her fall.

"I'll water your mount for you, Elieana," said Philen as he took the reins from her.

"Thank you, Philen, I am so tired my legs will not obey me," said Elieana.

"I know how you feel, Elieana, I had a hard time standing the first time I dismounted but in time we will both get used to it."

As Elieana listened to Philen she noticed he seemed changed, confident.

"Why don't you sit down, and I'll bring you some water," said Philen.

"I will. Thank you, Philen," Elieana sighed and gratefully hobbled over to a large tree at the edge of the clearing, away from the group of men. Her legs felt like they were stretched, never to be straight again. She wanted some time alone to recover from their long ride and not have to talk to anyone. She sat down beside a huge root extending out from the trunk of the tree, leaned back and closed her eyes. She was aware of her surroundings for only a moment and then fell asleep to the sound of birds chirping and the gurgling of the nearby spring.

Chapter 7

Jacq, on the run from his most recent employer, watched the two soldiers walk across the beach to the spot where he had met the guard the night before. He stamped his foot in anger. They were spoiling his plan, to go back and retrieve the sword for Girard and, he hoped, a second chance as an apprentice. These two men were making his task very difficult indeed.

He watched as they unearthed the body, wrapped it in a tarp and loaded it onto a cart. The boy with them, Jacq felt sure he knew him; he had seen him before when he had scrounged for food at the castle kitchen.

Jacq ran to the gate archway where he could hide in a doorway. He pressed his body into the darkest corner, waiting for the cart to pass. The boy, walking behind the cart, looked directly at him. Jacq could just make out the boy's face and recognized him as the son of Gaspar, the stable master. At first Jacq thought the boy saw him but he displayed no sign of recognition.

Once the cart rounded the corner Jacq left the dark safety of the arch and followed at a safe distance. They were taking the body to an undertaker. He dashed down a narrow alley and took a short cut to the street of the undertakers. There he found a spot where he could watch for the cart, unnoticed.

A short time later the cart turned into the street and proceeded until it stopped in front of a little building with a smaller stone hut beside it. Jacq circled around, running down the alley behind the buildings. His opportunity at hand; he could hit the boy on the head and search the cart for the sword, which must be in the cart with the body. He crept closer and closer when suddenly, a huge hound, lunged at him, barking crazily.

Jacq nearly fell over from shock. He ran back in the direction he had come from, tripping over some pots stacked in the alley. When he stopped running he leaned against a wall, panting, his heart pounding in his chest. He slid his body down the wall and sat on the ground then rested his head on his knees until his breathing slowed. While he sat there, he replayed the events of the last day in his mind.

It was curious, the guardsmen were being so cautious. Should they not report the events to the King? He thought there must be something he had missed but he couldn't think what it might be? Getting nowhere in his pondering when he heard voices and spied the two soldiers walking past without the boy and the cart.

Jacq leapt up with renewed energy and ran back down the undertaker's street, this time avoiding the alleyway. When he got to the cart he searched it thoroughly but found no sign of the sword, just the empty scabbard.

Jacq crept up to the building beside the cart and peered through a crack in the door. The boy he watched earlier sat on a stool; the body lay on a slab beside him. Jacq could not see the sword inside either. Just as he turned to leave he tripped on the doorstep and fell flat on his face. "Oh, why did I let my greed take over?" he whispered to himself. "Why did I want to leave the gong pit? I'm not cut out to be a spy." Angrily he kicked at the step, hurting the bottom of his foot. Rather than hurt himself further Jacq decided it would be better to follow the soldiers, so he hobbled down the street, in search of them.

When Jacq finally saw the two men again they had just split up; Darec, going to the officer's quarters and Jorian in the direction of the barracks. Jacq hid in an alleyway, while he waited for the two men to return. They passed by, a short time later, heading again towards the street of the undertakers. Determined to find out why they were being so secretive, he followed them again.

Just before he crossed the small bridge connecting the old and new towns, Jacq spotted one of Girard's men, lounging next to a tavern. The man blocked the only route he had to get back to where the soldiers left the body. Fearfully, Jacq slunk away, knowing death awaited if Girard's man discovered him.

He circled through the narrow, winding streets, until he passed a bath house. It occurred to him, if he cleaned himself up, perhaps Girard's men would not recognize him. Just as he reached out to open the bath house door, it opened, and out stepped Girard.

An unpleasant sneer spread across Girard's face as he descended the stairs. He grabbed Jacq about the throat with one hand. "You are a dead man," Girard growled at him and reached for the knife on his belt. Jacq spluttered. He couldn't breathe because of Girard's tight grip on his throat. His arms and legs flailed in every direction. Girard lost his grip and Jacq fell hard onto the cobbles, slamming his head on a stack of barrels.

"Master, one moment before you take my life," he croaked, rubbing his neck where Girard had squeezed it. "I have found what you seek."

Girard's eyes narrowed, thinking Jacq stalled so he could get up and run.

"I give you my word," he panted.

"Your word is worthless," snarled Girard.

"I know where it is. I have been following the men who have it." Jacq felt like crying he was so frightened.

"Tell me what you know, quickly now, before I slit your skinny little throat."

"The guard I killed last night," he whispered, "I buried his body and the sword in the sand far out on the beach. They found him and have taken his body to clean it. They are being very secretive. There is something else that is happening. When I find out I will report back to you, I give you my word."

"And what of the sword, where is it?"

"One of the men has hidden it. I will get it back for you."

Jacq groveled in front of Girard. He expected, at any moment, to receive a killing blow, instead he received a sharp kick in the ribs, knocking the breath from his lungs.

"See you get my property back and find out what is afoot before tomorrow's light, then I may see fit to spare your life," said Girard and he kicked Jacq again then stomped off, leaving Jacq sprawled, face down in the dirt.

When he caught his breath, Jacq crawled behind the stack of barrels and retched, shocked that all he received was a rib-bruising kick and not the death blow he expected. Using the side of the building for balance, Jacq pulled himself up and staggered off towards the castle, limping from the excruciating pain in his foot and holding his arms over his ribs to stop the sharp pain in his ribs every time he took a breath. He found a small alcove between the officer's quarters and the kitchen, where he could hide, a good vantage-point, to wait for the soldiers to return.

A commotion awoke Jacq sometime later. He saw the bulky form of the cook at the door to the officer's quarters, demanding to see the Captain of the Guard. A short time later the larger of the two soldiers he had followed earlier appeared and spoke to the cook. The soldier left immediately, staying in the shadows, as he crossed the courtyard.

Angry with himself that he had fallen asleep, Jacq silently followed the soldier, who passed through an archway and then climbed a narrow spiral staircase. Jacq climbed up the stair behind the soldier, keeping back far enough that the curve of the staircase hid him from the view of anyone looking down. He heard the soldier speaking to someone, but couldn't make out the words. Carefully he peeked around as far as he dared. The soldier stood on a small landing talking to the healer woman who stood just inside a doorway. The soldier's broad shoulders blocked Jacq's view of her face, but he knew her voice. She had cleaned a nasty cut on Jacq's arm soon after she arrived at the castle. Had she looked down she could have seen Jacq peering up from the bottom of the stairwell. The healer carried a travel bag and a girl with dark, curly hair, bundled in a thick blanket. After a short discussion, they retreated into the room and closed the door.

Jacq climbed the rest of the stairs and put his ear to the door. Much of the conversation did not make sense but with the mention of the Baltican King's daughter all the intricate pieces of the puzzle fell together. A sly grin spread across Jacq's filthy face. He felt giddy with excitement. The value of this knowledge, worth much more than the sword, would save his grimy neck many times over.

Jacq slunk down the stairs, looking back over his shoulder often, to confirm no one followed him. There would be many questions asked of him and possibly a stay in the dungeon if anyone found him there. Once free of the castle Jacq seemed to change and puff up with newfound confidence. He felt as if he owned the world. The closer he got to his area of the old town the more he swaggered. More than a few people noticed this change. Jacq the gong farmer, smelly little man, acting as if he owned the world. He attracted more attention than he should have. Someone rapped him on the back of the head and he fell like a stone.

* * *

Jacq awoke confused and dizzy. The room he lay in spun wildly. His head felt like it would split in two. He didn't recognize the room and he lay on something scratchy and hard. When he opened his eyes, he realized he lay on a rush covered, stone floor. A large wooden table with thick legs loomed above him. Large candles in brackets on the walls flickered occasionally, causing dancing shadows on the walls. At the end of the table he could see the legs and feet of a man, sitting at the table, eating noisily.

Sunlight filtered through a crack in one of the window shutters. Morning, he thought. He lay there watching the dust motes as they spun in the sliver of sunlight as he tried to remember what had happened that brought him to this room. He could only remember watching the soldiers on the beach digging.

Groaning with pain he slowly sat up and held his head with both hands. He massaged his temples, trying to stop the pounding and spinning in his head. Jacq licked his dry lips and coughed, irritating the dry membranes of his throat. He crawled over to a chair and pulled himself up to stand by the table. It came as no surprise to see Girard looking at him.

"Did you know, Jacq, you look very much like a ferret?" Girard motioned at him with the chicken bone he held.

A quizzical expression spread across Jacq's face, unsure if Girard expected a response. He rubbed the back of his neck with his free hand, the other locked in a death grip on the back of the chair. He coughed again, attempting to clear his throat.

“Water?” Girard asked.

“Yes, master,” Jacq croaked.

Girard pushed a goblet towards him.

Jacq took the goblet and reached for a water jug nearby. Full, cold and dripping with condensation the jug slipped as he poured, spilling water on the table. The puddle spread like a bloodstain on the dark wood. The sight startled him, making his hand shake as he poured, and the rim of the jug rattled against the edge of the goblet. Jacq's swagger and confidence had deserted him. He stood in this room, with a man who would easily order him dead. Suddenly he felt as if the roof was caving in on him. He felt sick to his stomach. It took all his strength to keep from falling to his knees and vomiting in fear in front of Girard.

He gripped the goblet with both hands and drank greedily, hoping the water would settle his stomach. When he finished he carefully set the goblet down and sank to his knees. The water he spilled dripped onto the floor, drip, drip, drip and the sound intensified in his aching head. "It must be the knock on my head that is doing this to me," he whispered.

Girard ignored him as he tore a chunk of bread, sopped gravy from his plate and stuffed it into his mouth. A little dribble ran down Girard's chin and Jacq gagged at the sight.

Jacq felt like such a coward then. Where had the confidence he felt disappeared to after discovering the daughter of King Stephan? It had left him as surely as an animal escaping through an open gate, to be replaced by cold, hard fear. He hated himself at that moment and realized what he was: a coward and a weakling. He sat there pitying himself then remembered the valuable information he discovered and which he hoped would save his life.

Slowly Jacq rose to his feet, gripping the back of the chair tightly. "Master, I have found some information that will greatly please you." He tried to deepen his voice, to sound more convincing.

"What, you have my sword?" Girard asked between bites.

“No, Master.”

“Then you will die for your error.” Girard wiped his mouth with the linen napkin lying beside his plate.

“Master, if I may speak.”

“Speak if you must,” he said, and flicked his hand at Jacq as if to dismiss him.

“Master, King Stephan had a daughter…”

“Yes, and she disappeared with her mother at the start of the war. Old news will not save you.”

“She lives, master.”

Girard glared at Jacq then stood, shoving his chair back with a loud scrape. He walked over and grabbed the collar of Jacq’s shirt and lifted him off the floor. “You lie to save your own neck,” he growled at him and squeezed Jacq's throat by twisting the collar of Jacq's shirt tightly.

Jacq gripped Girard's wrist with both hands as the collar slowly choked off his breath.

“No, master," he whispered, "I overheard the Captain of the King’s Guard and the healer. The healer has been living here with the girl for some time now. They left early this day in search of something but the girl, she is still here.”

“You will show me this girl this night and you may yet save your wretched life,” said Girard. He shoved Jacq at the same time as he let go of his shirtfront, causing Jacq to land heavily on his backside. As Jacq looked up at Girard a little seed of hatred grew in his heart. Girard then picked up his napkin and wiped his hands, a look of disgust on his face.

"Leave me. Clean yourself so I don't have to smell your profession on you. After the dinner hour, you will be back here to lead me to this girl yourself."

Jacq slowly rose from the floor, this time not using anything for support. He didn't want Girard to know he had caused him any more pain. He refrained from rubbing his buttocks which now likely had bruises from Girard's rough handling of him. Bowing deeply, he backed out of the room. As soon as he was outside he ran away as fast as he could, suffering from the ache in his back side and the burning from his bruised ribs as he did so.

Chapter 8

The sun sat low on the horizon when Jacq walked towards Girard's house. Freshly bathed he felt strange and uncomfortable, as if a mask had melted away with the water and soap. It seemed as if people noticed him more; he had no place to hide. He realized how bad he stank now that he could no longer smell himself.

The girl who drew the bath water for him, told him she did not think the sewer could ever be cleansed from his body. Later she commented that he cleaned up quite well. She even brought him clean clothes to put on. It seemed odd to him, a man leaving clothes behind. However, he had not complained about the gift. He hadn't had anything clean to put on for a very long time. In fact, he couldn't remember when he had ever had anything to put on that didn't stink.

Never had a girl come near him or even try to make conversation. He had felt extremely nervous when he gazed into her deep, blue eyes. She smiled, and a dimple showed in her cheek. He recalled how his whole body quivered and tingled when he paid for his bath and their hands touched. Embarrassed, he pulled his hand away, but in that instant, it seemed as if time stood still. In that moment, he had noticed so many things about her, the wisps of hair freed from the ribbon she tied it with; the creaminess of the skin at her throat; her small hand, rough from hard work. She had smiled again, bowed her head then walked to the back of the room to finish her cleaning.

Jacq had watched her walk away, his heart pounding but he had summoned his courage, and asked her name. She had looked back over her shoulder and smiled shyly. "Carlotte," she said, then flicked her hair back coquettishly, walking slowly away from him.

Amazed by this meeting Jacq walked back out to the street still thinking of Carlotte. Never had he felt this way before. This girl, beautiful in his eyes, had sweetness about her he never noticed in any of the girls he had acquaintance with. Although, he thought glumly, no nice girl ever wanted to come near me, my stench was so foul. When this business with Girard is over perhaps I shall find a different occupation, not Girard's apprentice but something else, something better. He again allowed himself one small glimmer of hope for a chance to make a new life for himself.

When Jacq reached the door to Girard's compound the guards did not recognize him in his new clothes, with his newly washed hair and the grime scoured off his face. The unmistakable odor normally preceding him did not give him away before he arrived. "I am here to see Girard," he told the guards.

"What business do you have with the Master of this house?" said one of them.

"I have a rendezvous with him this night. He has asked me to meet him here," said Jacq, enjoying the fact the men did not recognize him.

"There is only one who is to come here, and you are not him as he does not smell like a flower as do you."

A feeling of happiness welled up in Jacq's chest and a large smile spread across his face. "It is I, Jacq. I may smell like a flower but the man before you is Jacq, the man who meets Girard, this night."

Peering into Jacq's face the man grinned toothily. "You clean up well, my stinky friend. If you stay this way, we must give you a new name."

In an instant, the comment swept Jacq's elation away. Offended, he scowled at the man as he let him pass. I will get even with all of those who treat me as dirt, he thought.

"Go to the last door on your right, little man," the soldier jeered.

Jacq walked down the cobbled lane towards a courtyard at the end. The doors in the lane had no windows and no markings to indicate who lived there. When Jacq arrived at the last door he rapped once. The door opened, and a soldier reached out, grabbed Jacq by the arm, pulled him into a small entryway then slammed the door shut behind him with a kick of his foot.

"Who are you?" said the soldier gruffly.

"I am Jacq, here to see Girard," said Jacq.

"You will wait here until you are summoned. Do not move from this spot. When the Master is ready to see you, I will return and guide you to him."

While he waited, Jacq looked around the small entryway. He noticed a hatch part way up the wall, and looked inside. A refuse chute; inside, the spoiled remains of food splattered the door and the chute. The door beside the hatch, he guessed, led to a kitchen by the sound of clanging pots and aroma of food cooking. His mouth watered from the delicious smells emanating from the room. His stomach growled loudly, reminding him he hadn't eaten since the evening before.

A wooden stairway led to the upper portion of the house. At the top, he could see a thick, rich looking carpet and a heavy, elaborately woven drapery tied back by a thick golden rope. He had never seen such richness as this. Curious, Jacq cautiously climbed up to the first turn of the stair and peeked down the hallway. He saw the menacing gaze of Girard staring back at him from a large portrait on the wall. His heart jumped in his chest and he scrambled back down the stairs two at a time. When he reached the bottom, he stood rooted to the spot until the guard finally came back for him.

The guard motioned with a jerk of his chin for Jacq to follow him down a dark, narrow hallway. At the end of the hall they descended a steep flight of stairs where a door stood ajar. The guard motioned for Jacq to enter. Now so afraid of what might happen, Jacq started to retch. He felt dizzy and reached out to steady himself. When his hand touched the cold stone wall it felt like death to him. Impatiently the guard shoved him through the door and there, waiting in the dimly lit room, sat Girard at a small table. A sense of déjà vu hit Jacq. He felt as if he again stood in his little hovel, with Girard, after he discovered the sword missing from the sack.

Girard smiled but no mirth showed in his dead looking eyes. He crooked his finger for Jacq to come closer. "Well, Jacq, I hardly recognize you," said Girard.

"Yes, Master," Jacq croaked.

"Are you ready to show me this person of interest?"

"Yes, Master," said Jacq and he turned back towards the door.

"No, Jacq, we have another way we will go. And mind, I better be satisfied, or I will slit your throat."

Jacq felt his bowels threatening to empty on the spot. His knees felt like water. Thankful for the solid presence of the table, he leaned on it heavily.

The guard opened a small door on the opposite side of the room. Girard rose from his seat and went through. The guard grabbed Jacq's arm, shoving him forward, then followed behind him. Passing a torch to Girard he shut the door and locked it, then hid the key in a small crevice above the door.

The loamy scent of freshly dug earth hovered thickly in the tunnel.

"Where does this tunnel lead, Master?" said Jacq, trying to keep his voice from quivering.

"Back to the castle and under the guard's noses," Girard said. The pleased grin spreading across Girard's face looked demonic in the flickering torchlight.

They walked single file, Jacq sweating with fear and chilled to the bone. He now believed as soon as Girard had the girl he was no longer of any use; Girard would kill him. He would never accept him as his apprentice, ever. Jacq tried to push from his mind the thought of himself floating face down in the filth of the sewer. Not a lenient man, Girard punished his men severely when they made mistakes. Jacq knew that telling Girard about the girl only delayed him rotting in a rubbish heap. He intensely regretted coming. He should have just left the city to find a life somewhere far from Pelagos. Jacq decided then that if he got out of this mess alive he would leave Pelagos as fast as he could. He didn't know where he would go or what he would do but he knew he had to get as far away from Girard as he could while he still had his head attached to his body.

The short tunnel ended at a small door which did not keep the strong odor of the sewer out. The guard unlocked the door, held it as they went through then locked it and again hid the key above the door. Jacq suspected Girard had his plan, whatever it was, in effect for a long time. It also occurred to Jacq that they used him as a pawn, an expendable pawn, to bring Girard's swords into the city. If the swords were discovered, they had no fear of their plan being revealed because until that point Jacq had only spoken to a shadow. He could not identify anyone, then. He now could identify Girard and that, Jacq realized, was a guarantee of his demise.

They walked in the sewer until they came to another door, also new, no slime clung to it, as it did on the walls of the sewer. The soldier unlocked the door revealing another freshly dug tunnel. Jacq felt the confines of the tunnels stifling. He felt like screaming and desperately wanted to get away. The guard again locked the door behind them and with the clink of the key in the lock Jacq felt the chance of escape slipping away. They walked about a hundred feet more then came to a brick stairway leading up to a trap door. They climbed the stair and entered a large room. A glimpse outside, through a crack in the boards covering one of the windows, Jacq realized they were a stone's throw from the castle kitchen.

They were inside the wine merchant's shop, Jacq realized. Rumor had it the old man died unexpectedly. Soon after he died the new owner boarded up the windows. After that no one really paid much attention. A new sign would replace the old and it would be as if the wine merchant never existed. Jacq wondered then if someone in Girard's employ helped the man expire before his time. He had no doubt if Girard wanted something to look like an accident he had someone in his employ to carry it out.

The dim light from torches hanging on the walls of the courtyard outside filtered through the boards covering the window. The thin, white sliver of the moon guaranteed an abundance of shadow outside to conceal their movements once they left the building.

Girard handed Jacq an old woolen cloak to cover himself. It smelled of sweat. Funny, Jacq thought, as he draped the cloak over his shoulders, I never would have noticed the smell of sweat before.

The two men silently slipped out of the building. They slipped along in the shadows of the castle wall, moving silently, like deadly wraiths, towards their destination. Before climbing the stair leading to Elieana's chamber, Girard grabbed Jacq from behind. He pulled him back, deeper into the shadow of an archway. Girard pushed a dagger up under

Jacq's chin. The point of the dagger punctured Jacq's skin and he winced in pain as a thin trickle of blood slithered down his neck.

"This had better not be a trap, or you will die," Girard whispered into Jacq's face, the smell of onion heavy on his breath.

Nodding, Jacq grasped Girard's hand and pulled it away from his throat.

"I have told you the truth, Master. It is no trap."

He managed to express indignation when he spoke although he trembled. With trepidation Jacq turned his back on Girard then led the way towards the spiral stair where he had seen Darec and the healer woman talking. As they walked silently through the shadows Jacq reached up and wiped away the blood from the cut on his throat, scowling as he did so, and hating Girard even more.

Jacq ascended the steps to Elieana's chamber in front of Girard. Girard took no chances. Jacq knew as soon as they took the girl, Girard would have no difficulty sticking him with the dagger. What better way to dispose of Jacq than leaving him there to be discovered? The guards would assume the nameless men took her, would probably round them all up and throw them in the dungeons without a question.

They proceeded up the stairwell, no guard stood outside the chamber. At the top step, they paused, listening for sounds from inside. Jacq tried the latch, but it was locked so he lightly tapped. They waited for a few moments, but no one answered. A trickle of sweat ran down the side of Jacq's face and into the neck of his shirt, chilling him. If they do not answer, he thought, I die on this spot, tonight. Jacq tapped again, this time more urgent and louder. A chair scraped across the floor inside. They could hear someone moving, then the turn of the key in the lock. At that moment, Girard pushed on the door as hard as he could. The person on the other side of the door, knocked off balance, fell to the floor with a loud thud.

The two men entered the room and saw a large woman laying sprawled on the floor, attempting to get up. Girard went to her side but instead of helping her up he hit her on the head and she flopped back down with a grunt. Jacq watched from the doorway, shaken by the violence. He glanced over at the girl sitting up in her bed, wide eyed. Everything had happened so fast she didn't even have time to scream.

Girard reached into his pocket as he moved towards the girl. In one fluid motion he pulled out a piece of cloth and a bottle of liquid. He quickly poured the liquid on the cloth and just as the girl opened her mouth to scream Girard clamped it over her mouth and nose.

Riveted to the spot in fear, Jacq watched the girl grasping at Girard's hands, her legs kicking out as she tried to get away. Slowly her kicking and grasping subsided as the liquid on the cloth did its work. The whole matter took just a few moments but to Jacq it played out in slow motion and lasted an eternity. He twisted the cloth of his cloak in his hands, he had only wanted a little money, so he could get himself out of the gong pit. Never did he think of kidnapping to escape his old life. What if Girard killed her, he thought frantically?

Suddenly he lunged towards Girard and grabbed at his arm, trying to pull him off.

Girard looked at Jacq over his shoulder, a fearsome sneer spread across his face then he reached over, grabbed Jacq by the throat and threw him back against the wall. Jacq landed on top of the woman sprawled on the floor. He recognized her as Aldred, she worked in the kitchen. She was kind and often gave him left over morsels of food when he went to the kitchen begging for food. Revolted at the thought of landing on the unconscious woman he struggled to get to his feet. He didn't know what he should do but realized Girard cared little for anyone or anything and to Girard, Jacq's life could easily be squashed out like an annoying insect.

His fading usefulness to Girard occurred to him again. He realized Girard had no intention of letting him go or inviting him into his organization. That he let Jacq think of himself as an apprentice was just a cruel jest, at Jacq's expense. The realization his life would soon end finally sunk in. He must get away from Girard before they reached the wine seller's stall.

"Get up, Jacq," growled Girard. "Help me wrap her in this blanket then we will carry her back to the tunnel."

Jacq managed to climb over the unconscious woman and obeyed Girard. They wrapped Nada in a blanket and then carried her out of the room and down the stairs, Jacq at Nada's feet and Girard at her head. She weighed little, Girard could easily have lifted her. Jacq rightly assumed this was Girard's way of ensuring Jacq would return to the wine seller's stall with him. Once there Girard could dispatch Jacq anywhere he pleased. What better place than the sewers where no one would find him?

A cold shiver ran though Jacq's body, he feared, more than anything, dying down there in the cold, rank depths of the sewers. When they reached the darkened archway Jacq saw his chance, he dropped Nada's feet and ran as fast as he could through the archway and into the shadows beyond. Girard could not call out and he could not follow him. Jacq did not stop or look back. He ran as if pursued by demons until he found a hiding place in an alley, behind some large barrels, far away from the wine seller's shop.

Girard spared but a moment to watch Jacq run away then he hefted Nada over his shoulder like a sack of vegetables and headed towards the wine shop. He reached it with time to spare. When he was safely inside, noises outside caused him to peer through the boards on the window. A small group of soldiers approached the stairway to Elieana's chamber. They had come to take King Stephan's daughter to a chamber in the castle, to ensure her safety, until her father arrived for the wedding. They escorted a covered palanquin carried by two men with four soldiers marching two to a side. Girard cursed Jacq. A few moments longer and the soldiers would have discovered him with the girl. Girard resolved then that he would not rest until the ferret, Jacq, was dead.

Girard and the soldier, who carried the girl, sped back through the tunnels to Girard's residence. He ordered the guard to place a pallet on the floor for her to sleep upon then pulled out a small flask and gave it to the soldier. "Three drops of this in a jug of water. We don't want her waking and alarming the servants." Girard left his man to deal with the girl and stormed up the stairs, angry that he was almost discovered.

The soldier, a look of disgust on his face mumbled to himself, "It's not my job to be a nursemaid to a child." He kicked the door shut and locked it, leaving the key in the lock and Nada lying on the floor wrapped up in her blanket while he retrieved some straw for a palette, a water jug and a soil bucket.

Girard searched out his most trusted lieutenant, Arturo, to carry a message to Vasilis of the discovery of the girl. When Arturo walked into Girard's large study, a sly smile spread across Girard's face and he nodded for Arturo to close the door. "Arturo, this message cannot be written down and I trust only you to carry it to Vasilis, you will tell no other. Take the fastest horse from the stables and ride to Castle Delvar. Tell Vasilis, King Stephan's daughter lives. I have her in my control."

Arturo's brow raised in surprise at this news. Girard now had an extra measure of leverage. A vicious looking smile marred his face. Vasilis would stand to benefit from the girl's demise because his son, adopted by King Stephan, would be named heir to the Baltican throne in her stead. This news that King Stephan's daughter lived could be very profitable indeed.

Chapter 9

Nada awoke hours later, cold and shivering, in a small room lit only by a torch hung high up on the wall. The light wasn't strong enough to chase the shadows from the corners of the room. She lay on a straw palette with only her blanket wrapped around her. Confused, scared and shivering, she burst into tears. What happened to Aldred, she thought? Where were Elieana and Darec now? Who brought her here? The questions tumbled into her mind, but she had no answers, she couldn't remember.

She got up from the palette and limped across the room, careful not to set her injured foot down on the dirty floor. There were no windows. She tried the door, but it was locked. Crestfallen she sat down on the single chair by the table and poured herself a drink from a jug of tepid water.

An awful smell lingered in the cold, damp room. She pulled her blanket tighter around her shoulders and as she drank her memory of the past few days tumbled into her jumbled thoughts. She slashed her foot; Darec and Elieana went somewhere together; Aldred came to stay with her and then a man, those men came into the chamber. She spoke aloud just to hear her voice. "The man knocked Aldred down then grabbed me. He put a stinking cloth over my nose and mouth, I could not breathe and now I find myself here. Who would do that? What kind of person would do that?" she shouted as loud as she could, and her voice seemed to echo in her ears as she spoke.

Suddenly the room started spinning. Nada's stomach heaved. She abruptly stood, knocking the chair to the floor in her haste. She stumbled to the soil bucket and vomited into it, her stomach heaving painfully as she gagged and retched. Nada shivered violently, the room now seemed even colder than when she awoke. Disgusted she wiped her mouth on a corner of her nightgown. Nada rubbed her hands vigorously over her face and then she eyed the water jug; she wanted to rinse the sour taste from her mouth, but the room spun so crazily that she didn't think she would be able to stand again. She crawled back to the palette, shivering with cold and fear and curled up on the straw. Nada pulled her blanket tightly around herself and then she passed out.

Chapter 10

Jacq remained hidden behind the barrels until people going about their daily chores forced him to move along. He didn't know where to go. No longer could he hide in the sewers and he didn't want to go back there in any event. He had no friends. He had no family living that he could seek refuge with. Despair threatened, its icy fingers seeping into his mind. When he was about to give up he thought of Carlotte, the girl at the baths. She was kind, perhaps she could help him. Even if she could help him find a place where he would be safe from Girard and his men for a little while, until he could leave the city.

He peered out into the street to get his bearings. The night before he ran without paying attention to where he went, ducking into alleys and climbing over walls, trying to lose whomever Girard had sent to follow him. He thought now Girard probably hadn't sent anyone after him the night before because he had his prize. Having the princess in his house, safe and secure, was more important to Girard. Jacq had no doubt that Girard would send someone to search for him and kill him just because Jacq could identify Girard, but he would probably have waited until daylight. Now was the most dangerous time for Jacq. He realized he had to be very cautious now. He needed to get off the street.

Jacq realized, as he gazed out at his surroundings, that he ran across a good portion of the city the night before. If he back-tracked a few streets he would find the bathhouse where he first met Carlotte. He slunk out from behind the barrels, keeping his head down and being careful not to show his face. He proceeded down the street in search of the bathhouse. Jacq ducked into an alleyway before he got to the building, deciding the rear door was a better choice.

He tapped lightly on the door, anxiously looking over his shoulder. Jacq rocked back and forth, nervously waiting for someone to answer. He took comfort that no one in this city really knew him because he always stayed in the sewers, gong pits or his little hovel. Anyone having the same profession as Jacq would not be here, standing on the back stair of a bathhouse. These thoughts gave him a little more courage. He tapped again and when no one answered he quietly let himself in. He closed the door without a sound and glanced down the narrow hallway.

Jacq found no one on the main floor so he crept up the stairs, peeking into the rooms. He continued looking until he finally found Carlotte on the third floor, sitting on a stool in a small, sunny alcove, eating her morning meal. It had not occurred to him he had been holding his breath until he saw her. She looked up, surprise on her face and went to speak but he put his fingers to his lips for her to be quiet. Leaning down he whispered in her ear,

"Is there someplace I can speak to you where no one will hear?"

She looked down at her plate, then back at him, then nodded and motioned for Jacq to follow her. She walked to the end of the hall towards two closed doors. Opening the left side door, she entered a small room, which Jacq realized must be where she slept. The tiny room held a narrow bed and a small chair. She entered first and sat down on the chair then motioned for him to sit on the bed. Jacq entered the room, quietly closing the door behind him. He stood by the door, feeling too uncomfortable to sit, especially to sit upon her bed.

"What is it that I can help you with, sir, besides running the water for your bath?" She wore a small, sad smile as if she expected something inevitable, considering she worked and lived in a brothel.

Jacq replied in a whisper, "No. Not that. I need your help. I know of no one in this city willing to help me. I have no family, no friends. You were kind to me when I came here before. I have done some terrible things and now I realize I will pay, probably with my life."

A voice in Jacq's head screamed at him for telling even that much to this girl he hardly knew but he could not help himself and before he realized it he told her everything, about wanting a new life; the swords; the death of the soldier; Girard and the princess. She listened without interruption, her eyes growing wider with alarm. At times, she covered her mouth to stop herself from exclaiming out loud. Exhausted from whispering and reliving all that had happened in the past few days he flopped down on the floor, his head in his hands.

"I only wanted to get a little money, so I could leave this city and go someplace far away from the stench of the sewers," he whispered. "I didn't mean to kill the soldier, it was an accident, I was so afraid."

"I will help you, on one condition," she said and patted his shoulder lightly. "I will help you if you take me with you when you leave the city. I do not want to stay here. It is only a matter of time before the Madam of this house will order me to do more than run bath water and scrub men's backs. I do not want to stay here for the rest of my life, a captive toy for strange men. If you promise me, you will help me get away from here, I will help you."

Jacq put his right hand over his heart and whispered, "I promise, Carlotte, if you help me I will take you out of the city, so you do not have to spend the rest of your days here. I promise."

Jacq reached out and she grasped his hand. At her touch his heart skipped a beat. He smiled at her, the first smile in a long time. He felt happiness in that one small moment, that one small touch.

"You can stay here for now; it will be safe," she said. "I know of whom you speak, he comes here regularly to see Mathilde, the Madam of this house as does his man, Arturo."

With a start, Jacq thought back to that day in the room near the sewers and the wicked looking woman; the day he escaped when they discovered the sword missing from the sack. "This woman, Mathilde, is she tall with long black hair?" asked Jacq. His voice quivered anxiously.

"Yes. Why?"

"I have seen her before, with Girard, the first day I escaped from him." Jacq's face had turned a sickly grey color and he asked, "Is this her house?"

"Yes."

Jacq realized then that Girard had walked out of this same bathhouse the day he choked him in the street. His heart sank. He felt as if he had walked into a den of wolves. "I have been so very stupid. Every step I have taken in the last few days was without thought. How could I come to a place Girard frequents, when searching for a haven?"

"Do not worry," said Carlotte. "What better place to be than in the one place where they would not think to look for you?" Carlotte squeezed his hand, attempting to reassure him. "One other thing before I help you," she said.

He looked up at her, fear and distrust marring his features, "What is it?"

"I do not know your name. I cannot keep calling you, 'Sir'."

"Ah...Jacq," he stammered. "Jacq, my name is Jacq."

"Well, it is very nice to meet you, Jacq. Now, I must go to my duties. My day is only just begun. Have you had anything to eat today?"

Remembering he had not eaten since the day before, he shook his head that he had not. His stomach growled at the mention of food and Carlotte looked at him in surprise.

"I will get you a plate of food, because if not, your stomach will give you away," she jested.

That seemed to put him at ease somewhat, but he had difficulty recognizing humor when no one ever jested with him before.

"I thank you," said Jacq and he stood so she could leave the room. As she squeezed past him, he caught the comforting smell of soap and the musky scent of her body. In that moment, he realized he needed someone to hold in his arms, to feel her body close to his. His arms ached to touch her, hold her, but that intrusion was too great, especially here. She seemed so young. It would be a tragedy for her to remain working in this house and become a whore. Just the sound of that word left a bad taste in his mouth. Jacq felt a warm glow in his chest, he had never felt this way before. Perhaps this one purpose could help him become something other than a gong farmer, destined to live below the city in stench and filth.

As Carlotte shut the door she put her finger to her lips. Nodding, Jacq sat on the chair to await her return. A short time later he heard a faint scratch at the door. Carlotte carried a plate of food and pushed a canvas bag through the door with one foot. "I have brought you some breakfast," she whispered. Then she pushed the bag further along the floor, so she could enter the room and close the door. "There are some fresh clothes in the bag for you. Before you eat take off your clothes and I will clean them for you. I can believe you have been in the sewer tunnels again," she smiled, dimples showing on her cheeks.

Embarrassed, Jacq sniffed himself and made a face causing Carlotte to giggle and then quickly cover her mouth. "You are right, I do smell," said Jacq.

"We must be careful; the smell of the sewers travels with you. If Girard comes in and recognizes the smell, he will know you are here. I have lit some candles in the hall to disguise it, but I must clean your clothes right away to get rid of the odor.

"Quickly, undress before someone comes. I will soon have to draw water again. Once I am gone, you may rest on my bed. Do not leave for any reason, no matter what you hear in the hall. You should also know that the door right next to mine is a closet but there is a secret door at the back which will take you to the roof. You will find a small latch at the back of the closet, near the floor, on the right side. It will feel like a nail sticking out of the floorboard. Push it down with your foot and the door will spring open. Stairs lead to the roof. Once there, cross the roofs in a straight line towards the west, you will come to more stairs leading down to the street near the Mermaid Tavern. If, for some reason, you must leave in a hurry, take that route, do not go back through the house. I will be back as soon as I am finished drawing water for the tubs."

Carlotte turned her back so Jacq could remove his clothes. He pulled the clean ones out of the canvas bag and stuffed his soiled ones inside. Passing the sack back to Carlotte he took her hand, just for a moment.

"Thank you," was all he said because he felt tongue tied and breathless in her presence.

She nodded and left the room, closing the door quietly behind her. Jacq sat staring at the door, listening to her footsteps receding down the hallway. He stayed in the room throughout the day, at times dozing, at times craning his neck to see outside, fearful of getting too close to the window in the event someone in the street looked up and saw him. He heard no noise in the hallway to interrupt his thoughts.

This was the first time Jacq had ever sat still and taken the time to evaluate his life. He saw greed and selfishness. He thought about all the times that he committed thievery or been mean or lied. He did not like what he saw and now he had to include murder in his list of crimes.

Jacq was very tired, but he could not fall completely asleep, hounded by guilt ridden dreams because of what he had done on the beach. He lived with a lot of guilt and regrets but none so much as the regret for killing the young guardsman.

It was quite different to have a guilt-ridden dream, awaken and convince himself it was just a dream then go about his normal day. Now as he sat he could think only of the events of the past few days and the people he had crossed paths with. He thought of Carlotte, she needed no reason to be kind. Even if he said he could not help her he believed she would help him still. She only asked for a chance at a better life. Jacq understood this desire more than anything else and determined to make it happen for her, no matter what. Shortly after he had come to that decision Carlotte arrived with a quick scratch on the door.

"Jacq, one of Girard's soldiers is in the bath house. I just drew his water and he is quite drunk. I heard him muttering something about a girl. Could that be the girl Girard kidnapped?"

"Most probably it is. What did he say?"

"Just that he wasn't a nursemaid for a sickly little brat."

"Did he say where they are keeping her?"

"No, but I can find out."

"Be careful, Carlotte, these men are very dangerous. I do not want you to be hurt."

This sounded like a selfish thing for him to say, being dependent upon her good will. She looked as if she suspected selfishness from him.

"No, Carlotte, please be careful, not for my sake but for yours. You are so good and kind. I am concerned for your safety. Please, be careful."

A smile touched her face but only for a moment. It was not a smile that lit up her face and eyes as she had done before.

"I will, Jacq, be careful, I mean. As soon as I have found out anything I will come back and tell you. Girard is also in the house, with Mathilde, do not leave the room for anything. He is very angry."

She left the room again, the lingering presence of her return, the clean smell of soap, remaining to mark her presence in the room.

Chapter 11

When Carlotte returned to the room a short time later her distress was palpable. Her hair had escaped its pins and its disarray matched her mood.

"Is it quiet out there?" asked Jacq, concerned about her agitated state and a growing red mark on her cheek. She shook her head and silently looked at herself in a little mirror hanging on the wall.

"There is nothing much to tell," she said as she fixed her hair again. "Customers come in, some want more than a bath." Her voice came out in no more than a whisper as she spoke. She didn't turn around to face Jacq, she just stared at her reflection in the mirror and then it suddenly the mirror cracked and fell to the floor.

Jacq looked at the broken pieces of the mirror laying at Carlotte's feet and then looked at her. He didn't think she had touched it and wondered how it was that it fell to the floor but then Carlotte interrupted his train of thought.

"I did overhear Girard and Mathilde talking, but about nothing important."

Carlotte bent and carelessly began to pick the shattered pieces of the broken mirror off the floor.

"Be careful, you will cut yourself," said Jacq.

Carlotte looked down at her hand and watched as a drop of blood slowly trickled down her hand and then dripped onto the floor. She wiped her hand on the hem of her dress and then returned to fixing her hair, but her hands shook so that she couldn't pin it back up.

Jacq slowly approached Carlotte and gently turned her around to face him.

"I must have bumped the mirror," she stammered. The red mark Jacq had seen earlier had spread and taken on the appearance of a hand across her cheek. He touched it gently but said nothing. Carlotte rested her face against his hand then large tears welled up in her eyes.

"The guard who came with Girard tried to touch me. I pushed him away but then Mathilde noticed and accused me of eavesdropping. She slapped me on the face."

Anger boiled up inside Jacq. "You don't have to take that from her."

"I do," said Carlotte. "I am her servant. She houses, feeds and clothes me. I am indentured to her for a very long, long time, still."

Her head hung down in despair and when she looked up her face had transformed into a tragic mask. She looked nothing like the girl he just met and admired for her courage and gentleness. She seemed broken somehow.

"Mathilde told me that if I had so much free time to stand around eavesdropping she had more engaging work for me. She will force me to do what I fear most; to start working as a whore in this brothel.

"This evening, I must begin working as a whore. She has arranged an appointment for me with one of her most regular customers." A heart wrenching sob shook her body. She wrapped her arms around her belly then laid down on her bed without another word. She faced the wall and when Jacq reached out and touched her arm she flinched as if his touch scorched her.

Anger replaced Jacq's earlier fear. He would free Carlotte as well as the girl he helped Girard kidnap. The thought of either of them being under Girard's control was unthinkable. The underground room was the perfect place to keep the girl until Girard could somehow get her out of the city. Instantly Jacq devised a plan. It will be easy for me, thought Jacq. I know the sewers; we could escape that way without anyone seeing us or knowing which direction we went.

"Carlotte, I have a very dangerous idea but one I think will work. I will help you get away from this place and I will get the girl away from Girard. I believe I know where Girard is keeping her. Pack some things in a sack, nothing much, mind, just some food and some dry clothes for you and the girl."

Carlotte still faced the wall but Jacq could tell she was listening. "Jacq, we have to do this before tonight. How can we..." her voice trailed off.

"We will be doing it right now. Go find yourself some men's clothes and something for the girl to wear. We are leaving as soon as you are ready."

"But Jacq, we don't know where she is."

"I think I know exactly where she is. We will take the chance of finding her and then we will escape with her. Come, we must hurry. Find the clothes and I will explain on the way."

Carlotte rolled over and sat up on the edge of the bed and wiped the tears from her face. Jacq reached down and grasped her gently by the shoulders. "You will no longer work for Mathilde. We will escape together and find a new life for ourselves outside the city. We will go somewhere where no one will know us and live happily; without fear." Jacq helped Carlotte rise from the bed then opened the door for her to go gather the clothes and food.

"Hurry back," he whispered and gave her a little push out the door and closed it behind her. When he was alone, Jacq leaned back against the door wondering if he had lost his mind. Could he run back to the lion's den with someone he had begun to care a great deal about? If this plan did not work, Girard or Mathilde would kill them both; Girard, for this betrayal or Mathilde for stealing her property.

"Enough," he whispered, "It must be done. If I am to do one good thing in this world it will be to save Carlotte from her fate here in this house. If we find the girl perhaps I will save my soul somewhat for killing the guard."

Carlotte came back a little while later with Jacq's still damp clothes and a water proofed canvas bag which contained a loaf of bread, a large piece of cheese, some dried meat and a stone bottle of wine and the extra clothing for the girl, if they found her.

Once Carlotte changed into Jacq's clothes they exited her tiny room and entered the closet in the hallway. She pushed the latch and a narrow door sprung open, leading to a steep and narrow flight of stairs. She ran to the top of the stairs to another door and again pressed the latch with her foot, but the door would not budge.

"It won't open," she whispered frantically.

"Let me," said Jacq as he squeezed past her.

"Where is the latch?"

"On the floor, slide your foot to the right, you will feel a nail sticking up."

Jacq slid his foot along the floor until it snagged on the nail. He pushed on the nail and the door at the same time. The door bumped against something. He shoved again, and the door opened a crack. He shoved again and again and then they heard a loud thump and the sound of something rolling. The door flew open, crashing against the wall outside. Jacq stumbled out, off balance from pushing with all his weight on the door. At the same time, he caught sight of a large barrel rolling off the roof. Angry voices hollered out from below. They heard a crash and a man cursed loudly. Carlotte's fear of being discovered ignited.

"Mathilde's rooms are on this side of the house. If she is there, surely, she will have heard the crash," whispered Carlotte.

Almost at once they heard Mathilde's angry voice shouting at the men in the street and demanding what was going on.

"Mathilde, someone must be on your roof and has knocked down this barrel, it almost hit me and look what it has done to my cart," a man shouted. "You will pay for my cart, Mathilde, and all my damaged goods as well," shouted the man.

The sound of the window slamming shut frightened Carlotte more than anything. Frantically she tugged on Jacq's sleeve.

“We have to leave now. She will send her men up here, they will catch us.”

Jacq grabbed her hand and pulled her through the door, “Lead the way, hurry now.”

Carlotte and Jacq ran across the tops of the adjoining roofs and across a narrow plank connecting two rooftops. After crossing the plank Jacq stopped long enough to pull it away from the other roof. Knowing their pursuers would not be thwarted for long he hoped it might give them a few extra minutes to get away.

“There!” someone shouted. “There they are, get them,” shouted a big, burly man running towards them across the rooftops.

“Hurry Jacq,” Carlotte screamed.

She ran as fast as she could, Jacq running at her heels. As they dodged around the corner of a taller building Jacq heard someone shout, “That’s Mathilde’s girl running away. Who is she with? When we catch you,” he yelled, “You’re a dead man.”

Jacq cringed. Now that people knew Carlotte had run off she would have nowhere in the city to hide.

“How much further, Carlotte?” he gasped, as he caught up to her.

“Just about another hundred yards, there are stairs leading from the rooftop to the tavern below. If we can get there then we will be safe for a time.”

Jacq doubted they would be safe even for a few moments. They had to hide immediately.

"Carlotte, is there a way to get back to the castle kitchen from here? Near the wine merchant's shop?"

"I don't know if there is a way, on the roof tops, but if we climb to the street now we can run back that way," said Carlotte.

"Do you think we can do it without being seen?" asked Jacq.

"Maybe not, I think it is too far," said Carlotte.

Jacq looked to the street below and recognized the Undertaker's Street where a nearby trap door led into the sewer.

"Here, we can get down here," said Jacq as he climbed over the edge of the roof.

Carlotte followed him to the roof edge and watched as he climbed down a rickety drainpipe. The loose nails holding it to the wall pulled out further as he moved downward, causing the pipe to sway dangerously, threatening to throw him to the ground.

"Climb down Carlotte. I will catch you if you fall," said Jacq.

She looked over her shoulder to see if anyone followed, searching for another way to get down but upon hearing their pursuer's voices shouting she promptly climbed over the edge. When she got to the bottom they ducked back under the first-floor overhang of the building just as their pursuers passed by overhead. Carlotte's heart pounded in her chest and tears threatened to fall. She closed her eyes tightly, blinked and took a few deep breaths to calm herself.

Jacq grasped her hand, then tugged her forward to follow him. They jogged quickly down the street, passing by the building where the soldiers took the body of the dead guardsman. At the end, they came to a narrow lane leading behind a tiny tavern where they found the trap door. It wasn't locked, there was no need, none but the gong farmers used this door.

“I’m sorry, Carlotte, our escape must be through here.”

“I’m trusting you Jacq," her voice trembled. "You promised to help me; I'm counting on you now.”

Jacq opened the trap door and the repugnant stench of their escape route wafted up at them. Carlotte glanced anxiously at him as he held the door up then she stepped down onto the first rung of the ladder. When she reached the bottom, Jacq climbed in, shut the door quietly and slid down with not a moment to spare as one of their pursuers gazed down into the street from the rooftop above.

Chapter 12

A spark flew up from the flint Jacq struck against the wall giving him a quick glimpse of the tunnel, so he could get his bearings. In some of these older tunnels torches hung on the walls so the gong men could light their way. Jacq walked slowly forward, striking the flint as he went until he found an old torch hanging from a rusted sconce on the wall. The torch was damp, so Jacq ripped a strip off the bottom of his shirt, wrapped it around the top then lit it.

"Try to stay on the ledge, Carlotte, so you don't get your feet soiled."

Carlotte obeyed, nodding her head rapidly. She didn't reply because she had her hand clamped tightly over her mouth, was holding her breath and pinching her nostrils tightly. When she couldn't hold her breath any longer she breathed in with quick, panting, breaths.

"Not much further," said Jacq. He looked back at Carlotte and saw her hand clamped tightly over nose and mouth. He felt a twinge of annoyance but then pushed the thought from his mind. In all his years in the tunnels he had learned not to notice the unbearable stench. How he achieved that feat he did not know. Since he had washed a few times in the last few days the foul reek turned even his iron clad stomach with disgust. Even now Carlotte did not complain which said much for her character.

They came to a small door. Jacq stuck his fingers in a little crevice above the door and pulled out a key. He remembered the guard placing it there when he helped Girard find the girl. He unlocked the door and they entered a newly dug tunnel. They ran to the next door. Again, he searched for a key above the door. He carefully pushed the door open, peeking through the crack to ensure no one was inside. They crossed to the door of the little room where he met Girard.

There on the floor lay the young girl, covered with a blue blanket. The room smelled of vomit. Jacq tried to wake her up, but she slept soundly. The clink of metal on metal attracted his attention and he turned to see Carlotte pouring herself a drink.

More loudly than he intended he shouted, "No! Do not drink that. Girard uses drugs and poisons. This girl must be drugged to not wake. Look, I can pinch her, and she still sleeps."

Carlotte carefully set the cup down, keeping her eyes on his face. When she let go of the cup it teetered and fell to the floor with an alarming clang.

"Jacq, where are we?" she said, her voice coming out in a shrill squeak.

"In a secret room under Girard's house."

"But how are we to get away from here?" She tucked her hands under her arms to stop their trembling.

"Back through the tunnel from where we came. That will be the most secret way."

As they discussed how they could get the girl away they heard someone singing a raunchy tavern song in the tunnel, their only escape route.

"Carlotte, quickly, lock the door to the tunnel. The key is there on the table."

Carlotte ran into the hallway and locked the door moments before someone on the other side tried the latch. The man banged on the door and shouted angrily for the door to be opened.

Terrified Carlotte ran back to the room. "Jacq, it is the soldier from the bathhouse I told you about. The one who complained about being a nursemaid. Jacq, what are we going to do?"

The banging and pounding on the door increased and then the sound of loud thuds as the man threw his full weight against the door. The heavy door withstood the heavy pounding but the latch, not so strong, started to loosen and bend. Realizing the danger Jacq started to drag the table towards the door.

"Help me move the table and chair against the door to block his way. Our only escape now is through the house."

Carlotte's face blanched with fear. "Jacq, surely someone inside the house will catch us. How will we explain this?"

"We won't be explaining this to anyone. I have a plan, but we haven't a moment to lose."

Jacq didn't know yet how he could achieve their escape, but he needed to let her know he had control of the situation. Together they moved the table and wedged it against the door then they draped the girl's arms over their shoulders and ran up the stairs.

The banging stopped but Jacq felt certain the guard had gone to find help, probably to save his own skin rather than stopping the girl from escaping. Now they had to go through the house, carrying the girl.

Tempted to leave her there, he was about to say so when Carlotte said, "You know there really isn't any reason to save this girl. The danger is great, but I admire you for trying to make right a wrong. I'm proud of you, Jacq."

Had Carlotte not said she was proud of him, they could be running for their lives this very minute without the heavy weight of the sleeping girl. It irked him that he felt this way, his old self, thinking only of himself. He wanted to change. He ignored the tiny voice in his head telling him to flee and save himself. "Hurry, Carlotte," he picked up the pace, more to complete his task and overcome his fear than anything else.

They went as fast as they could up the narrow stone staircase leading to the entry where Jacq first waited to see Girard. He motioned for Carlotte to set the girl on the floor. Jacq opened the door a crack and peered into the entry. A kitchen worker stood by the open trap door, throwing food scraps down the waste chute. Jacq realized the chute was large enough for Carlotte and the girl to fit in, they could escape that way.

He whispered to Carlotte, "You and the girl are going to escape through the waste chute in the entryway opposite this door. I think that it goes to a large compost dump for the farmers on the other side of the wall. You should have a soft landing. I will not fit through, so I will go back through the sewer and find you on the other side of the wall."

He believed his chances of completing this feat on his own without being caught were slim, but he had to convince Carlotte to leave with the girl. He liked Carlotte very much and didn't want anything to happen to her. The only way he could get her to escape through the chute was to convince her he had another plan for his own escape.

"Wait here," said Jacq. I will get you something to slide on. When I tap on the door come out with the girl."

He silently opened the door, again checking to make sure the kitchen worker had returned to the kitchen. He silently climbed the stairs in the entryway and pulled down the draperies hanging across the stairwell. The drapery poles fell with a crash but at this point he didn't care if someone heard. The kitchen noises were loud enough to muffle the sound and he would take his chances if others in the house heard and came to investigate.

Jacq ran down the stairs two at a time and rapped on the door. Carlotte came out, dragging the girl by her arms. They wrapped the girl in a cocoon of drapes, lifted her limp body up and slid her dead weight into the chute feet first. A little push and down she went. Jacq had a fleeting fear of her waking up screaming as she slid down, but she made not a peep. He felt sorry for her; from the strength of the sleeping potion she would be very sick when she awoke.

Carlotte wrapped the second drape around herself and Jacq lifted her into the chute. She reached up and gently touched his cheek. "Thank you," she whispered and then slid away out of sight.

Jacq reached for the door so that he could escape through the sewers, thinking the guard had left but he heard someone coming from both the stairwell to the tunnel and from the alleyway outside. Without a second thought, he dashed up the stairs.

Chapter 13

Carlotte flew down the chute and out of the drapery but luckily the damp, greasiness of the chute let her slide without scraping all the skin off her backside, her elbows taking the only beating. She shot out of the opening and landed in a squishy pile of refuse narrowly missing the girl sprawled out where she had landed, still soundly asleep. Carlotte's entry into the world on the other side of the wall disturbed a flock of sea birds roosting on the refuse bins causing them to squawk in displeasure.

"Surely someone will come, and we will be captured. Be quiet, stop your clamor," she whispered loudly and waved her arms at the birds. They flew off, squawking, leaving Carlotte sitting on top of the odorous pile of compost which the farmers in the nearby village used to fertilize their fields.

Carlotte mumbled to herself, trying keep her fear at bay. Enclosed on all sides the large wooden bin had thick, wooden slats spaced far enough apart to let air in but no animal to pass through. She was safe for the moment. Separated from the noise of the city Carlotte listened to the sounds outside of the bin. She hadn't heard the songs of frogs or crickets since she arrived in Pelagos such a long time ago. A comforting sound. She thought about what she faced now. She had no place to go. It was a fearsome place away from the heavily fortified and walled city but right there, sitting in the bin, listening to the evening songs of frogs, it didn't seem so fearsome.

Many years past, before the land had been settled and walled, large animals roamed freely. Huge cats, larger than a horse, enormous herds of herbivores and strange creatures with striped hides and massive curved horns made their home on this fertile plain. Early settlers hunted the animals until their populations were decimated or driven back into Sangan through the Guardian Pass in the Barbicon Mountains. After the ancients blocked the pass no one in Pelagonia or Baltica ever saw any of those animals again, their existence now only recalled in bedtime stories.

The most fearsome place was Sangan. No one from the Kingdoms of Pelagonia and Baltica traveled there because of the cruelty and violence of the Sangans. Most adventurers who traveled into Sangan didn't return, but those who did told amazing stories of huge flying birds and the herds of animals covering the wide, flat plains. They told of a land of grass; of immense trees with small villages high up in their branches, well out of reach from dangerous predators.

Most people believed the stories were just the ravings of madmen, having lost their minds from lack of food or water or from traveling and living rough for too long. Other travelers told of huge cities built high on steep, rocky mountainsides to protect the inhabitants from large carnivores. They even told preposterous stories of large birds with Sangans riding on their backs. She smiled and shook her head at how ridiculous it seemed.

Sounds of a struggle on the opposite side of the bin interrupted Carlotte's thoughts. She crawled across the squishy heap to help the girl who had rolled to the side of the bin. The drapery entangled her upper body and she couldn't move. She whimpered and called out for help to someone named Elieana.

"Don't worry," said Carlotte, attempting to calm the struggling girl as she uncovered her face. "You will be all right. What is your name? Do you hurt anywhere?"

"My arms won't move. What happened? Where am I? What is that awful smell? Nada, my name is Nada. Who are you?" she mumbled. "Help me. Help me, the man..."

Carlotte helped Nada to sit up and pulled the drapery down off her shoulders, causing her to shiver in the cool night air.

"Wait here," said Carlotte, and she went in search of her bag of clothing and food. She slogged across the bin, trying not to think about the slime, and what the lumps and bits of bone had been before being dumped there. She helped Nada move to the edge of the bin, so they could climb down. Nada had little strength, probably from the drugged water, thought Carlotte, thankful that Jacq had stopped her from drinking it.

Carlotte used the drapery as a sling and lowered Nada to the ground, the distance of the height of a tall man. Carlotte climbed down using the spaces between the slats as a ladder. Once on the ground Carlotte found a small tool shed where she could leave Nada until she recovered fully from the sleeping drug then she walked a short distance away from the shed to contemplate what she should do next.

Surprised that no one came to investigate after the bird's loud squawking Carlotte then thought it highly unlikely anyone nearby would have great concern for the contents of the bin. Now that she stood on solid ground she tried to figure out where to go. Should she stay and wait for Jacq? How long, she thought, would it take him to get out of the city? The city gates were probably closed now, Jacq could not leave until morning. Girard would have plenty of time to put the pieces of this puzzle together and be looking for Jacq and Nada. She wondered if anyone would link her disappearance with Jacq but then doubted that as the guards took up their pursuit far from Girard's house.

Perhaps they would think Nada had gotten out of the house herself. Briefly she felt pity for the guard left to watch over her. From what she now knew of Girard, the man would not be long for this world for letting her escape.

The missing draperies, she thought, might be a clue to their escape route. Even though they may not think of the chute as an escape route Carlotte felt she should leave the vicinity as soon as possible, it would soon be dark, and she would not be able to find her way to search for a safe place to hide unless she searched as soon as possible. Also, with the rising of the sun the chances of Nada being discovered in the shed increased so Carlotte ventured out in search of a safer place to take Nada and wait for Jacq to find them.

On the opposite side of the road a high hedge separated the farmer's homes from the road. The hedge served to keep any breeze blowing across the bins from wafting the smell of them towards the village, but they also obstructed the view of the road should someone peer out their window.

Carlotte followed a path leading off the road. She pushed the shrubbery aside and the calm water of a tiny bay, sparkling in the setting sun, greeted her. She walked out onto the deserted beach. A tiny boat house stood at the end of a narrow, rickety dock. A huge, rusty lock hung on the door. The boards on the boat house and dock, rotted with age, proved they had not been used in a very long time. She picked up a rope lying on the dock which disintegrated as soon as she moved it. She doubted anyone used this area to bathe, most people she knew avoided putting even a toe in the water for fear of attracting creatures from the deep.

Carlotte did not fear the sea, she respected it. Growing up in Girona, a small village to the south of Pelagos, she had observed the large creatures with long necks and large paddles for feet as they hunted for prey in deep water. More fearsome for her, the stories of the Fish People who kidnapped young children. Frightening to think of as a child but now she didn't believe a word. First, how could ordinary people breathe underwater? And second, no one that she knew had ever seen one. More likely, she thought, the stories were to frighten young children from going near the water.

Investigating further, Carlotte found a tiny cave, overgrown with creepers, perfect to keep them dry and out of sight. They could stay there for a short time. She hoped Jacq would find them, she didn't know how she could leave a message or a clue for him. She went back to the tool shed and found Nada standing up with her arms crossed, her mouth set in a grim line across her face.

"Who are you and why have you brought me here?" demanded Nada attempting to make her voice sound menacing.

"My friend knew you were taken to that room. He feared for your safety and wanted to help you," said Carlotte.

"Only three men knew what happened to me, the fat soldier left to guard me, the man who drugged me and a skinny little man who came to my chamber. Which one is your friend?" Nada tried to make her voice sound menacing and tried to sneer when she said the word friend.

"His name is Jacq," said Carlotte. She realized what Nada was attempting to do and made herself be as kind and gentle as she could be.

"I don't know him."

"No, you don't. He told me the man that took you might harm you."

"Jacq is the skinny little man who came to my chamber isn't he," said Nada angrily. "You don't have to answer me. I know I am right. The man who took me from my chamber was cruel and hateful. He put the foul-smelling cloth over my face. The soldier he left to guard me was just as bad. He grumbled when he came to the room and said I should not be his problem, so who else could it be? I saw this Jacq person in my chamber. Why did he help the other man? Who is that other man? What does he want with me?"

Nada spoke quickly, attempting to keep her emotions in check but her voice started quivering as she choked back her tears.

"The other man pushed Aldred, she fell on the floor and didn't get up." Nada wept silently and Carlotte put her arms around her.

"Please don't cry. Jacq is my friend. He is helping both of us. He did take Girard to your room in the castle and then afterwards realized his mistake. He is very sorry for it. He has promised to help me leave the city, but he wouldn't leave until he got you away from the big man. Girard is his name. You are right, Girard is very cruel."

Suddenly a dog barked in the village, startling them.

"We must leave this place Nada. It isn't safe, one of the villagers could find us. Can you walk?"

"Yes, but I need help because of my injured foot. If I can lean on you I will be able to hop."

"Put your arm around my waist. I found a place where I think we will be safe until Jacq comes." Carlotte wrapped the damp, pungent drapery around them and with their arms around each other they hobbled down the road to the little cave and, Carlotte hoped, safety.

Chapter 14

Jacq ran up the stairs of Girard's house two at a time. Convinced Girard would suspect he was responsible for the girl's disappearance, the best thing, the only thing he could do was to make it seem as if thieves ransacked the house. He hoped this might deflect Girard's fury from him to some unknown person. He did as much damage as he could as he ran down the long hallway; pulling down Girard's portrait; smashing vases and making enough noise to draw attention away from the refuse chute.

At the end of the hall a door stood open to a large, richly decorated room. Large portraits hung on the walls, men and women wearing odd costumes and holding large bows and spears. Jacq ran across the room, flung open the windows then rifled through the desk, leaving the drawers open and gaping with their contents strewn across the floor.

A sheet of parchment fluttered to the floor, catching Jacq's eye. He only had time to read the first few words 'assassination of King...' then the sound of angry voices in the hallway sent him scurrying to the window. Soldiers stood in the street below, blocking his escape. He had nowhere to run.

Frantically he looked around the room for a place to hide. Cabinets and bookshelves lined one wall. He dove inside the cabinet furthest from the desk. Just as he closed the door the sound of heavy footsteps entered the room. The man shouted. Jacq recognized Girard's voice and his muscles tensed. He felt like a mouse waiting for a cat to pounce on him. More footsteps thudded into the room.

"Find Jacq, the gong farmer," Girard roared. "He did this. Bring him to me. I'll rend his bones. There will be nothing left of him. And find Arturo, he should have returned by now from his errand."

Girard slammed his fist on the desk. The sound of a clipped, yes sir and then retreating footsteps mingled with the sound of Girard muttering as he slammed drawers shut. Girard closed the window and with the click of the latch Jacq's chest tightened.

Footsteps moved toward the cabinet where Jacq hid. The cork on a bottle popped and liquid splashed into a goblet. Jacq licked his dry lips. An enormous bang on the countertop above startled him, causing him to bump his head. He broke into a cold sweat, waiting for the cupboard door to open. Girard growled, his deep voice making Jacq quake.

"I know you've been here Jacq; I smell your stink. I will rip your heart out, when I find you." Girard's voice grated on Jacq's nerves like the shrieking of rusty metal. He leaned his head against the wall of the cupboard trying to control his breathing, preparing himself to spring out of the cupboard should Girard open it. For just a moment he thought of Carlotte and what would happen to her and the girl if Girard caught him? They needed him. A grim smile crossed his face. They needed him and here he sat, stuck in a cupboard.

A chair creaked as Girard sat, letting Jacq know that he had moved away from the cupboard. At least he knew that Girard would not find him for a few moments longer. Girard spoke aloud as if Jacq stood in front of him, belittling him, questioning him. “What were you looking for, Jacq? Money? You looked in the wrong place, gong farmer. Now if you had opened my liquor cabinet," he said then chuckled a subterranean chuckle that rattled Jacq's bones.

A tentative knock on the door interrupted Girard's mutterings. “What is it now?” growled Girard. "I don't want to speak to anyone until that ferret is found."

“Master, one of your guardsmen is here, requesting a word. He smells like a stable yard or worse. Will you see him here?”

“No, in the boot hall, it stinks badly enough in here already.”

Girard’s footsteps crossed the room and the door closed. Jacq breathed deeply then opened the cupboard door a crack to ensure no one remained in the room. He climbed out and stretched to loosen the cramping in his muscles then he looked at the liquor cabinet directly above where he hid from Girard. He opened the doors and saw an ornately decorated box, covered with gold filigree. Inside the box sat a red leather pouch. He looked over his shoulder as if he expected to see someone watching him then he picked up the pouch and shook it. The pouch jingled with the rich sound of gold then he stuffed it inside his shirt.

“Time to get out of here,” he whispered, and he ran to the window. The street below was dark and silent, the guards having moved on in their search for him. Jacq stepped out of the window, balancing himself on the narrow ledge. He pressed his back against the wall and inched his way along the ledge, shuffling sideways until he reached the corner. When he rounded the corner, he saw stone balconies with metal railings lining the wall of the opposite building. The buildings were close together, so he launched himself across, grabbing the railing on the opposite side before he plunged to the street below. He skinned his knees and hung there for a moment wincing in pain then slowly pulled himself up onto the balcony. He used the spaces between the bricks to climb to the roof. With only one slip he reached the rooftop where he rolled over onto his back to catch his breath and settle his pounding heart.

Jacq stared up at the stars. Funny, he thought, I have never taken a moment to do this, to look at how beautiful the night sky is. I wonder how different my life would have been had I lived it up here rather than crawling in the filth underground? He shook his head to stop his dreaming, he had to decide what to do next.

At this point he did not want to move hastily and get into worse trouble. He needed to get out of the city. Carlotte had told him about a trail to the water's edge by the Mermaid Tavern. If he took that route he could walk along the beach until he came out on the other side of the wall. That way he could avoid moving through the city altogether and hopefully find Carlotte in the farmer's village. Girard's men were probably searching the streets and sewers for him. For that matter, they could also be on the rooftops, but he would have to take his chances.

He peeked over the edge of the roof to the street below. He saw no movement and no windows to Girard's rooms on this side of the building. Suddenly from Girard's house a man's voice screamed out his name.

"Jaaaaaaaacq."

Certain Girard had just discovered his leather pouch missing Jacq slinked away, across the rooftops, towards the Mermaid Tavern. There would be an even greater pursuit of him now that the money pouch was missing. Jacq stayed in the shadows as much as he could, thankful the moon was but a sliver in the night sky, determined to get to the tavern before his cover of darkness faded away with the morning sun.

Jacq made his way across the rooftops in a circuitous route. He had to go to the street a few times because there was no other way to pass between some of the buildings. At times, he saw the king's soldiers marching through the streets, but they didn't seem to be searching, just making their presence known. He didn't feel as threatened by their presence as he did by Girard's men who searched the alleyways thoroughly. They were an ominous presence. Jacq hid behind barrels in alleys, inside broken-down carts and once missed being caught by Girard's men when he started to climb down from a rooftop. If a dog hadn't barked at the men walking through the alleyway they would have heard him as he scrambled back onto the roof. The delays and re-routing cost Jacq much time and when he finally found the stairs near the tavern the sun had just started to rise.

Jacq peeked over the roof edge and saw the opening in the bushes where the pathway led to the shore. Now or never, Jacq plucked up his courage once again and he took the steps, two at a time. His shoes clattered as he ran down the stairs but being so close to his goal he didn't care. He burst from the stairway and sprinted across the narrow, cobbled street and into the bushes without stopping.

Jacq hid in the bushes at the side of the road, peering out as he breathed a sigh of relief that no one came to investigate when he ran down the stairs. He began his descent down the rocky, winding trail to the shore. From his vantage point on the top of the trail he could see the top of the Samos Falls, breathtaking as the water fell from the cliffs. His new life, he thought in wonder, an opportunity to journey throughout the land and visit beautiful places. He would have enjoyed just sitting and gazing out at what he could see of the falls, but he knew he must hurry to find Carlotte and the girl and get them to safety.

The steeply winding path was slippery and treacherous with vines and the odd twisted tree clinging to the cliff face. He had to slide on his backside at times because of the steep descent and his ill-fitting shoes, which kept falling off. At the bottom of the trail he found a narrow, pebble-strewn beach. Jacq could smell his body after the exertion of his flight from Girard's house. When he found Carlotte he didn't want her to think of him as a smelly man so with his new care for cleanliness he walked to the water's edge and scrubbed his face and arms in the salty water then carefully picked the grit from his skinned knees. The salt stung but he didn't mind, thankful he had finally escaped his old life.

The wall to his left spanned the top of the hillside, separating the beach where he stood, and the inlet that the Samos falls emptied into. As he planned his route around the edge of the wall he glanced back up the trail. A movement at the top of the trail caught his eye and he watched to see if he could make out what it was. Someone stood there but he couldn't make out who it was and didn't want to wait and find out. He needed to get away. He couldn't go to his right as the beach circled back towards the castle with a sheer cliff face that plunged into the water. On his left, the beach rounded the point, becoming very steep with jagged rocks in the water below. It looked to be an easy climb at the point, but he had to get there by going through the water. He physically shivered at the thought of entering the water and imagined something lurking below the surface, waiting to snatch him by the legs and drag him under.

Jacq glanced up at the trailhead again and saw more people, some were already a third of the way down to the beach. He now recognized the King's Guard by the color of their doublets, dark blue with gold trim. Believing Girard reported the stolen money, arrest and death awaited him, especially as he carried the evidence in his pocket. Jacq had no one to speak in his defense. There had never been anyone to speak for him. No one cared for the loss of one gong farmer and no one would believe his story about the girl. He could delay no longer and dashed into the water. Luckily it wasn't any deeper than mid-chest as he waded towards the rocks. Jacq could not swim but fear of being caught by the guards overpowered any other fears he had, and he kept going. He kept his eyes focused on the rocks at the point and his mind on Carlotte and the new life they could have together.

When he reached the rocks, he pulled himself along until his body floated in water over his head. Panic crept into his mind as he remembered the horrible stories his father told him, of the sea creatures swimming in the deep. Surely his splashing would attract something. He gasped raggedly, he did not want to drown. The more he thought of those stories, the more fearful he became, the harder his heart pounded. He pushed on as fast as he could go over the slippery rocks. Twice he lost his grip and his head went under. He popped back up gasping and coughing up the salty water that filled his nose and mouth and stung his eyes.

The pounding of Jacq's heart drowned out everything, including the shouts of his pursuers. He focused only on his destination, the tip of the hillside where the rocky slope became less steep and jagged. Jacq looked back to the beach one last time. The men who pursued him were running out of the water. Suddenly an ugly, pointed, black head, on a long, sinuous neck, snaked up out of the water. The creature's mouth gaped wide, revealing rows of long, wicked looking teeth. The creature snapped at the nearest fleeing man, just missing him. The man screamed in fear and ran as fast as he could through knee-high water. The creature snapped again, again missing its prey then it threw up its head and let out a long, loud, warbling cry. The creature's red eyes suddenly noticed Jacq clinging to the rocks. It paddled backwards and sank slowly beneath the water, only the head remained visible, its eyes fixed on Jacq as it glided towards him.

Panic ripped through Jacq's mind and he struggled to get higher up the cliff wall. The rocks slashed his palms and feet and a trail of blood marked his passage. He looked back to where he last saw the creature and at that same moment the head struck out in a sinuous arc. Jacq scrambled sideways and the gaping, tooth filled mouth narrowly missed him. The creature struck out again and again, but it couldn't get close enough for a strike because of the submerged rocks at the point. With one last burst of energy, Jacq pulled himself up and around the edge of the cliff. The creature followed, striking out again, shrieking. Jacq felt its stinking, fishy breath. He screamed and scrambled higher up the cliff.

Thwarted, the creature let out a terrifying shriek and sank back into the water. It floated beneath the surface, staring up at Jacq as he clung to the rocks. Jacq waited, for what seemed like hours, in the merciless sun for the creature to leave. Finally, Jacq scrambled sideways across the cliff face inch by inch, ripping his nails and fingertips until they bled. After he climbed clear of the water he slithered down off the rocks onto a tiny, sandy beach. He staggered well away from the water and fell face forward in the shade of a dilapidated shed.

Chapter 15

Carlotte awoke to a man's terrified screams, intermingled with other more terrifying sounds, which sent chilling shivers running up and down her spine. The hair on her body rose, tingling her skin. Whatever was happening she didn't want to know. She huddled closer to Nada, pulled the soiled drapery tightly around them then stuck her fingers in her ears. She hummed a silly song to drown out the sounds. When she thought she could bear it no longer she heard a blood curdling scream, a warbling screech, then silence.

She sat huddled close to Nada for a long time and then finally, she removed her fingers from her ears and listened. She could hear the scrabbling sound of rocks falling and that sound frightened her even more. Afraid of what might be outside the cave, her cocoon of safety, she hugged Nada closer and fell into a troubled sleep. Her last thought, why did Nada sleep through it all or were the sounds just a figment of her imagination.

When Carlotte awoke again she strained to hear any noise outside the cave. Finally, she gathered up her courage and peeked out through the vines. The warmth of the sun on her face and the tangy smell of salt off the water comforted her and instantly made her think of her home in Girona. She saw no movement on the beach, so she crept out to stretch her cramped muscles. The cove seemed safe now, but she remained alert, expecting someone or something to pounce on her. She would not easily forget the screams and warbling screeching which left her feeling jumpy and nervous.

The Samos Falls to her left rumbled as it fell onto the rocks at its base. Even though she could not see the falls the spray rose into the air above the hillside and to her great delight bright little rainbows sparkled over the water. On her right stood the shed and the rickety little dock. The beach extended past the shed, ending at a cliff face and the trail leading back to the farmer's village.

She wandered about examining the shells and pebbles covering the beach then walked to the water's edge to wash her hands and face. The desire to be clean tempted her to take off all her clothes and swim but fear of the creature screaming during the night prevented her. When she finished her bathing Carlotte sat down on the sand. The gently lapping water and the sparkle of sunlight on the surface mesmerized her. It was a luxury she had not enjoyed for a very long time, to be able to sit without worrying about being slapped or worse. For the first time since arriving in Pelagos she allowed herself to daydream. As the water gently lapped against her toes and the sun warmed her face the terror of the day before and the screams during the night seemed not so frightening anymore.

"Probably some fish or animal," she spoke aloud. She stood, brushed the sand off her legs and walked back towards the cave to check on Nada but as she turned she caught a glimpse of something laying beyond the shed. Her heart thumped wildly in her chest and her first thought was to run, thinking perhaps it was the creature she heard screaming. The object moved, and she realized it was a man making futile attempts to rise off the ground, but he collapsed face down onto the sand once more. Cautiously she approached him. The man's arms and legs were covered with blood, insects buzzed around the open wounds. She rolled the man over, causing him to groan in pain, and recognized Jacq's face through the matted hair and sand.

Gently Carlotte smoothed the fine brownish hair back so she could look at him. He did not have a bad face. He had a wide forehead and high cheekbones with thick, dark brows. His nose was long and straight; he had full lips and reddish-gold fuzz covered his chin. She had thought him to be quite a bit older but on second thought they were much closer in age, perhaps in his twentieth year. Strange, she thought, how life brings people to certain places. She wondered how he came to be a gong farmer, the lowliest of occupations. He said he had no family, no one to turn to for help. She wondered what had happened in his young life that left him so alone.

As she admired his face Jacq's eyes shot open. He struggled and flailed his arms and at the same time stared at her, but seemed not to recognize her, then he sat bolt upright, hitting his forehead painfully on Carlotte's. He looked wildly about as if expecting something to come bounding out of the water then fell back, his head landing on Carlotte's lap.

Chapter 16

King Albryk slammed his fist down on the table, narrowly missing an expensive porcelain bowl. "What have you done with the child," he demanded, his voice burning with fury. He rose from his chair and paced back and forth in front of Jorian who stood rooted to the spot.

"She was resting in her chamber when I last saw her, My Lord." Jorian looked directly at the King. This was not a time to question himself and decisions already made.

"You will arrange to have her brought to my residence immediately," said the King.

"My Lord, there are many people in the streets, many strangers. Is it wise to move her in the daylight hours?"

"No. You are right," replied King Albryk looking directly at Jorian. "Move her after dark. Take a contingent of soldiers with you in the event there is trouble. It must be done this night with no further delay. My personal healer will attend to her when she arrives."

The King pulled a bell cord at one side of the room, summoning his chamberlain who arrived within minutes with a soft tap at the door.

"Enter," bellowed the King, a little too loudly owing to his concern that the long missing daughter of King Stephan was in his city. King Stephan might harbor ideas that Pelagonia kidnapped his Queen and his daughter. He could not allow that thought to take hold and destroy everything they had achieved to finally make peace.

"Sire, you summoned?" said the chamberlain.

"We have an unexpected guest who will arrive late this evening. Make rooms ready for her," replied the King.

"It will be done immediately, My Lord," the man bowed, exiting the room as silently as he had entered.

King Albryk fixed his eyes on Jorian, his expression conveying his memory was long, these events would not easily be forgotten. That they had not told him of Nada's existence as soon as they knew she lived in the city he would address after the treaty signing.

"You must be discreet. This will be done with the utmost secrecy; do you understand? No one must know of her existence until I have spoken to King Stephan myself."

"Yes, My Lord," replied Jorian, bowing deeply as he moved towards the door. Just as Jorian opened the door to leave the King called out, "When Darec Redford returns with the healer they will come to me before they brush the dust of travel off their clothes. Do I make myself clear?"

"My Lord, they will be told to attend to you as soon as they enter the outer gates." Jorian brought his right fist to his heart and bowed again. King Albryk nodded to Jorian then waved him out of the room.

After Jorian left, King Albryk filled a goblet to the brim with heavy, sweet wine. He drank it in one long swallow and gasped at the sweetness. Refilling the goblet, he retreated to an alcove and sat in a chair, placed so that he could gaze out the window. He set the goblet on a nearby table, leaned his head back and massaged his temples, another worry etched between his brows.

CHAPTER 17

Immediately after Jorian's audience with the King he ordered a small contingent of his men to move Nada to the castle in a covered palanquin. He ordered them to attend the chamber where she stayed, after nightfall, to ensure few curious onlookers. He instructed them to be unarmed but have their weapons at the ready in the event they met with any challenges by unknown citizens and dress as servants. They should look like servants, he thought, not warriors for there would certainly be questions by passersby if they saw armed men attending the healer's chamber.

Jorian sat in his office that evening, waiting for his men to report on their completed task. The light of a single, flickering candle gave the room faint light, too weak to chase away the gloom. His brooding upon the events of recent days enhanced his foul mood. There were too many questions without answers. He hoped that Darec and Elieana were well on their way to finding the proof of who Nada was. There were so many people whose lives would be changed because of Nada's discovery. Not many of them would be happy that she had reemerged, least of all the Princess Verenase.

Light taps at the door interrupted Jorian's ruminating. "Come," said Jorian somewhat gruffly.

The Sergeant at Arms opened the door slightly and stuck his head in before pushing the door open completely. His expression indicated he did not bring welcome news. He saluted, then waited for Jorian to speak.

"Sergeant Nitin, what news?" said Jorian.

"She was gone before we arrived," Sergeant Nitin said.

Jorian groaned inwardly and ran his fingers through his thick brown hair then nodded to the Sergeant.

"The woman caring for her was injured," said the Sergeant. "She told us two men barged into the room and knocked her unconscious. When she awoke, the girl was gone."

Jorian rose from his chair. "We will speak to her, perhaps she can shed some light on the identities of the two men." Jorian and the Sergeant left at once. Not a soul lingered in the wide square outside, the sound of their boot heels clicking on the cobbles were the only sounds disturbing the night air.

* * *

They found Aldred sitting in a chair in Elieana's chamber with a damp cloth over her forehead. When she removed it Jorian saw a large lump surrounded by an ugly reddish-purple bruise which spread across her forehead and down one side of her face.

"I am sorry Jorian." She shook her head in grief. "They barged in and knocked me flat. Before I could get up the larger of the two men hit me. When I awoke..." she covered her face with her hands and sobbed, "Nada was gone. I had not time to see what they looked like only that the man who shoved me was tall. They both had woolen cloaks on. All I can remember is a swirl of the black cloak and then nothing more."

"We will find her, Aldred," said Jorian. Go back to your chamber and rest. I will send word when we find her."

Trembling, Aldred rose from the chair. Jorian helped her down the stairs and watched her walk slowly across the courtyard towards her kitchen. When she reached her door, Jorian ascended the stairs to the chamber where the Sergeant waited for him.

"There is nothing to find here," said the Sergeant who had already searched the room. "No sign except this piece of cloth. I suspect they used it to subdue the girl before they removed her from the room."

"You are probably right," said Jorian. "Post extra guards at the gates tonight in the event they are still in the city. Start a search at once."

Jorian's men searched the city throughout the night but found no sign of Nada. The next day Jorian received a report of some citizens pursuing a man and a woman over the roof tops of the city. They also vanished without a trace.

While the search took place Jorian did not return to his home or to his room in the barracks. Sleep evaded him until finally, exhausted, he fell asleep at his desk, his head resting on his arms. A rap on the office door stirred him and for a moment he couldn't recall where he was.

"Enter," he rasped, his mouth dry and stale.

He drank from a goblet of tepid water on his desk, cleared his voice and repeated "Enter," loudly, as the knocking became more insistent.

The door opened and a soldier peered in.

"What do you want soldier?" his voice croaked. He swigged more water then wiped his mouth on his sleeve.

"Sir," the man saluted, standing stiffly at attention.

"Well, out with-it man," Jorian said irritably.

"Sir, a man was spotted climbing down from the roof of the Mermaid Tavern. He ran down the pathway to the sea at the base of the cliffs."

"Well, who was it? Where is he?" said Jorian.

"The fugitive ran into the sea. Some of my men followed him but a sea dragon attacked before they could reach him. I do not think the man survived."

"And how do you know he didn't survive? Do you have a body? Did you see him being killed?" said Jorian. He stood up and leaned over his desk and glared at the man who took one step back, intimidated by Jorian's aggressive response.

"No, Sir. They do not have a body, but they are certain the man did not survive. The beast attacked him as he climbed back up the cliffs." The man pulled at his collar nervously as his face turned a mottled red color.

"Did they see him being killed?" growled Jorian a second time in a very threatening manner, very unlike his usual easy-going character.

"The man did not survive because the beast attacked him as he climbed across the cliff face while trying to escape," the soldier repeated. "They reported to me they heard screaming.

The watch reported they heard much screaming and then nothing. Shortly after that the creature sunk below the water. When they felt certain the creature had departed, they did investigate the cliff side. They found blood on the rocks. They stopped their pursuit when they found the blood and no remains and then proceeded to make their report."

Jorian slammed the flat of his hand down onto his desk, rattling the objects sitting on top.

"Did you follow no further?" he questioned quite loudly.

"No, Sir. I was not with the watch, Sir."

"Did you go to the farming village to determine if the man climbed around to the other side of the cliff?"

"No, Sir."

"Well do it," he bellowed. "And report back to me before this day is through."

The soldier leaned back as if expecting Jorian to take a swing at him then he hastily saluted and backed out of the room, quietly shutting the door behind him.

Chapter 18

Jacq ran on and on, desperately trying to escape his pursuer. The hunter reached out to seize him, but Jacq turned and twisted, always escaping by a hairsbreadth. The hunter, eyes of red fire; huge teeth, sharp and yellow, dripping with poison, snapped again and again. Jacq's heart pounded in his chest painfully and his breath came in ragged gasps. The hunter snapped out again. Its breath hot and foul. He ran from the monster forever, it seemed, but a glimmer of light appeared, a soft voice calling his name. He knew the light meant safety. He ran until he could not take another step. Suddenly something grasped his arm. He raised his fists to fight. He struggled and flailed. He sat bolt upright and banged his head on something hard and then he fell back onto something soft. His head hurt but the sudden pain and headache seemed to knock some of the fog from his brain.

He could not comprehend immediately his surroundings but then he recognized Carlotte. She cradled his head in her lap and spoke soft nothing words to him as she rubbed her forehead. At first, he didn't understand what she said then as the dream fog in his mind lifted he slowly relaxed. The tension flowed out of his body and he lay there staring up into Carlotte's sweet, kind face and sighed deeply, "Carlotte, how did you find me?"

“After we fell from the chute we climbed down, and I left Nada, that is her name, Nada, I left her in a tool shed and searched nearby for a place to hide until you came for us. I found this beach and a little cave behind those vines over there,” Carlotte pointed in the direction of the cave. “We slept in the cave, but the screeches and screams awoke me. I was afraid to go outside.”

Jacq felt embarrassed for his screaming. “A sea dragon attacked me. I narrowly escaped. If the rocks had not blocked its way it would have eaten me in one gulp,” he blurted out, spittle spraying from his mouth as he spoke. Jacq wiped his mouth with his sleeve, grimacing as he realized how bad he smelled. He scuttled back slightly, self-conscious that Carlotte might smell the stench of filth and fear on him.

"I am sure that the creature making that noise was fearful to behold," said Carlotte.

Silently Jacq thanked her for letting him be brave.

“You escaped though. You are safe here,” she said, feeling very guilty for not venturing out when she heard the screams earlier. She patted his shoulder, attempting to calm him. “Jacq, I am sorry, I heard the sounds of the creature attacking you, it frightened me so badly I was too afraid to leave the cave. I could have helped you."

“Do not be sorry,” he panted. “You could have done nothing. The creature was enormous; its mouth full of huge, sharp teeth; its long neck, like a writhing snake. It could not reach me because of the rocks," he said and then hung his head, ashamed. "I think whoever pursued me will think it got me because of my screams.”

"Jacq, that beast struck fear in my heart and I only heard it from the safety of a cave. You were right there. You saw its teeth and huge mouth. You know what its intentions were. I am very glad you are safe. You were very brave." She patted his arm, trying to comfort him, unnerved by the telling of his harrowing experience and, she saw, greatly embarrassed.

Trying to change the subject from Jacq's escape it suddenly occurred to her to ask, "Why did you climb on the cliffs to get here?" said Carlotte.

"The King's men pursued me. I think Girard reported me as a thief."

"But why? What did you do?"

Jacq told Carlotte everything that occurred after she slid down the chute from Girard's house. She did not say a word while Jacq told his tale, only her facial expressions changed. At first Jacq expected her to be angry and she would think him a coward, but to his surprise she smiled.

"I think, Girard has provided you with the means to start your new life, Jacq," said Carlotte. She laughed softly.

He thought about it for a moment and then nodded, "You are right, he has. I have suffered much danger and fear because of his plans. He did not intend to pay me for bringing the swords into the city. Now I have received payment. Carlotte, will you come with me and share this life with me?" he asked shyly.

"I will, Jacq, but what of the girl, I mean Nada?"

Jacq had forgotten her completely and wasn't quite sure what they should do with her.

"We can ask her to come with us," said Carlotte.

He didn't want to consider taking Nada with them, but he agreed to speak to her. They both got up and walked arm in arm to the cave, Jacq leaning on Carlotte because of his battered feet. When they rounded the shed they saw Nada sitting on the soiled drapery which she had spread out at the mouth of the cave.

"There you are," Nada smiled at them and patted the drapery for them to sit down beside her.

"Nada this is Jacq," said Carlotte.

"Hello, Jacq," said Nada, appearing to forget how angry she was that he came to her chamber. She proceeded to set out the contents of their bag of food, as if they just arrived for a luncheon and she had not recently escaped from a dungeon through a refuse chute. Jacq took the piece of stale bread she offered and munched on it as he watched her, thinking her very unlike what he thought a princess should be.

Finally, Nada spoke up, directing her gaze upon Jacq. "Why did you rescue me?"

Her forthrightness surprised Jacq. At first, he thought her very innocent and shy. Now he did not know what to say. Carlotte and Nada looked at him, questioning expressions on their faces. He stammered and sputtered, almost choking on his bread.

"Girard..." Jacq sensed he had to be completely honest with her, though he didn't know why.

"The other man, Girard, he..."

"He hurt Aldred. I saw him," Nada blurted out. "I saw you too, but just for a moment before I passed out from the cloth he held to my face. He shoved you," said Nada.

"Yes, he did, and I fell on top of the woman."

"Aldred. Her name is Aldred," said Nada angrily.

"Aldred," said Jacq. "I don't think she was badly hurt," he said lamely, trying to lessen the impact of him hurting the woman.

Nada's lip quivered. He could see she cared very much for this woman, Aldred.

"Why did you come to my room that night? Why did Girard want to take me?" Nada demanded.

Astounded, Jacq realized Nada did not know her identity, where she came from. "Do you not know? You are a very important person," said Jacq.

Nada laughed, "Maybe to Elieana I am but not to that man, Girard."

"You are most important, especially to King Stephan of Baltica. You are his only daughter."

"I am Elieana's daughter. She found me in a broken carriage, no one else remained of the people I traveled with. My real parents are dead."

"She may have told you that," replied Jacq, "But she didn't tell you all. I heard her talking to the soldier, Darec. She told him you are King Stephan's long missing daughter and on that very night they left the city. I do not know where they went but they seemed to be in a great hurry to leave. I was Girard's apprentice," Jacq paused then, remembering that he was never Girard's apprentice. He corrected himself, "I worked for Girard and told him what I knew of their conversation. He planned to ransom you. When we arrived at your chamber I realized how wrong I was to help him. I feared for my life and escaped after he drugged you. I believe he planned to kill me after we took you from your chamber. I am sure of it. I am sorry, Nada, I only wanted a better life..." his words faded away, he felt wretched for his guilt and for telling her that he left her in Girard's grasp, without making a further attempt to rescue her that night.

Jacq felt like a whining dog, so he hid his face from her view. "Carlotte and I decided to leave the city, to help each other after I ran from Girard, but I could not leave you there alone at his mercy. We, Carlotte and I," Jacq looked over in Carlotte's direction. "We took the chance that Girard hid you in the chamber below his house, so we went there to take you back. Now it seems we have nowhere to go, the King's soldiers and Girard are searching for all of us."

"I know where we are," replied Nada.

"How could you possibly know where we are?" asked Carlotte. "It was dark, and you were still suffering from the effects of the drug when I brought you to this cave."

Nada read the look of surprise on their faces and felt as if they thought of her merely as a child. This angered her more than anything else. "I am not a child," she said, and she tried to keep her voice from quivering. "You do not believe me, but I have been here before with Elieana. She came to the Alatanian Grotto behind the falls. The Alatanians stay there with their young until they are old enough to go out into the sea. Their young were sickly, they sought Elieana's help. Could we not go to them and stay with them in the grotto until the soldiers have stopped searching?"

“You mean to stay with us?” asked Jacq. "Do you not want to go back to the castle to await the arrival of your father?"

Nada replied in a soft voice, trying very hard to hold back her tears. “Elieana is gone and she lied to me. I do not know King Stephan and why he didn’t search for me throughout all those years.” The unwanted tears ran down her cheeks and she hastily wiped them away. She would not let herself think that perhaps he had searched for her but because of the war it was very difficult for him to find her.

Jacq’s anxiety grew with this new situation, like a band tightening on his chest. His throat started to close, and he coughed to try and loosen the tension he felt. He could not keep the King’s daughter with him. How could he care for her properly? How could he keep her safe? He looked at Carlotte hoping she would say something to the girl to change her mind.

Carlotte saw the worry showing on his face; she wanted to help them both. She reached over and pulled Nada close and hugged her. “Nada, I am sure Elieana, your mother, will come back for you. There must have been a very important reason she left so suddenly. It must also have been very difficult for your father as well. The war, the grief for your loss.”

“She must have left because she expected to face punishment for keeping the King’s daughter,” said Nada. Once she spoke that thought out loud her grief overwhelmed her, and she began to sob uncontrollably, covering her face and curling up tightly into Carlotte’s embrace. In response Carlotte rocked her back and forth, all the while hugging her tightly, patting her back and smoothing her disheveled hair.

Jacq stood up and hobbled back and forth across the sand. He shook his head, distressed because he didn't know what to do. How could he get out of this situation? How could he get the girl back to the castle? How could he get away with his head still attached to his shoulders? How could he get away with this bag of money which accused him as a thief? The thoughts screamed in his head again he thought only of himself.

Suddenly he ducked inside the cave. He waited for his eyes to adjust and in the dim light he spotted a small crevice high up on the wall. He tucked the money bag inside the crevice and covered it with sand. It gave him some relief to hide the incriminating bag of money. One problem dealt with, but many others still troubled him, with no solutions at hand. Somewhat relieved he exited the cave and resumed his pacing. He needed to think.

In one of his turns Jacq faced towards the pathway leading from the beach to the village and saw the soldiers walk out onto the beach. He stopped and stared at them in disbelief. He glanced around in search of a place to run then slumped down on the sand. Trapped. No time to run and nowhere to run to.

Nothing in his life went as it should, this situation was no exception. The only positive aspect of this new predicament was the King's men found them and not Girard's. At least the King's soldiers did not slit the throats of their prisoners. He thanked the Goddess that the incriminating money bag sat safe in its hiding place, one less threat against his life and not a moment too soon. He also realized that the money bag would have incriminated Carlotte, even though she had nothing to do with its theft.

Nada struggled to break away from Carlotte's sudden tight grip. She turned to look at what Carlotte stared at and recognized some of the approaching soldiers. She wasn't sure if she was happy or sad that the soldiers found them. Her head hurt from crying and her face felt swollen, but she realized Carlotte and Jacq were in danger and maybe she could help them. She stood up, smiled happily and waved to the approaching soldiers. "Hello, guardsmen of the castle Pelagos, I am Nada, the healer, Elieana's daughter. Have you been looking for me?"

"Carlotte," Nada whispered, "Stand up," and she pulled on Carlotte's arm.

The surprised look on the men's faces when Nada stood and bravely faced them brought a smile to Carlotte's face. She stood up beside Nada and waved to the soldiers.

"We have been searching for you Nada. How is it you come to be here?" asked the Captain in charge of the search party.

"I will tell my story to Jorian, if you please," she replied. "My friends here have helped me. They must come too."

"They will come but under arrest," replied the Captain gruffly then he ordered one of his men to get a covered wagon from the village to transport the captives to the Hall of Justice.

The soldier thumped his chest with his right hand and then marched back up the trail, his boots kicking up little showers of sand as he walked. The Captain sent another soldier to report directly to Jorian the recovery of the persons they sought. A few minutes later the first soldier returned, slightly breathless, because of his size, as evidenced by the rolls of flesh wobbling under his chin.

"Sir, I have commandeered a cart from one of the villagers. It will be waiting at the trailhead to transport the prisoners."

"Thank you, soldier. They are not prisoners, at least one of them is not. Escort these two to the trailhead." He pointed at Carlotte and Jacq.

The sweaty soldier thumped his chest again then grasped Carlotte and Jacq by their arms and led them from the beach. Jacq's head hung low in defeat. Carlotte's face paled with fear and her lower lip quivered but she didn't cry as she stumbled along. When they reached the cart Jacq and Carlotte climbed into the back and then the soldier climbed in beside them. Sweat beaded on his forehead and little drips rolled down his cheeks. He pulled out a large pink handkerchief and mopped his face and brow. He seemed cheerful enough and remarked to no one in particular, how very hot it was.

A guard carried Nada to the cart, so she didn't have to hobble on her injured foot. He set her gently on the bench opposite Carlotte and Jacq then climbed in beside her. He glared at Jacq and Carlotte but didn't speak to them as he watched, with disgust, as the other soldier mopped his face.

When the cart started to move Carlotte shivered uncontrollably, cold despite the heat. She realized that her shivering caused the cart to shake and to control herself she grasped Jacq's hand tightly. She feared her return to Mathilde's brothel and couldn't stop thinking of the horrible future of servitude, of the worst kind, that faced her.

Jacq gruesomely focused on the forms of punishment he faced for the death of the soldier on the beach and the theft of Girard's money. When they finally reached the castle, he felt cold and clammy. His fine hair was pasted to his head from a combination of the heat inside the cart and his fear of the consequences. Carlotte and Jacq still held onto each other with a death grip, neither wanting to let the other go.

The cart soon passed under the archway to the city, from where Jacq had watched Darec and Jorian pass by with the body of the dead guardsman. The cart wheels rattled and bumped on the cobbles of the narrow streets then came to a stop. The guards did not move to get out; they just sat with their prisoners until another guard lifted the canvas flap. Jacq looked out at the doors of the Hall of Justice across the courtyard. Richly dressed men and women passing by stopped to watch. Jacq stared out at them as fiercely as he could, hoping they would turn away in embarrassment but they kept watching, their cold eyes showing their contempt. He shouted at them to turn away but all they did was laugh, their laughter echoed in his brain.

Jacq gazed around the courtyard with its benches and large pots full of colorful flowers. It seemed such a pleasant scene and a pleasant day, could this all really be happening to him, being arrested and taken to the dungeons? Why, he asked himself silently, did he try to change his position in life? No one in this courtyard would ever give him a second glance if he greeted them on the street.

The soldier who lifted the cart flap helped Nada out and then picked her up and carried her across the courtyard. Nada stared back towards the cart and watched Carlotte and Jacq. Carlotte stumbled but the guard stopped her from falling, grabbing her arm and twisting it painfully. Both looked very frightened but for some reason, at that moment, Nada felt nothing. She didn't care. The deep sadness she felt at her perceived loss of Elieana rested heavy on her heart. She never wanted to smile again. So much had happened in so few days; she didn't know where Elieana had gone; she wondered about King Stephan, the father she could not remember. She lay her head down on the guard's shoulder as tears of grief and sadness trickled down her face.

The guard, perhaps thinking Nada cried tears of joy at being rescued hugged her tight and patted her back to comfort her, his gentleness caused Nada to cry harder and a choked sob escaped her throat. She cried for the loss of her life with Elieana. She cried for the loss of her friends; for her lost freedom and running barefoot on the beach alone, with only her hound. She cried, fearful of the father she couldn't remember. She cried, and in those few moments Nada, the carefree sixteen-year-old girl disappeared forever.

Carlotte started up at the façade surrounding the huge doors of the Hall of Justice. The carvings adorning the walls and door frames showed men in judgment of others; men and women lying prostrate in front of the judgment seat, their faces etched with fear of the cruel and unyielding judges. Her heart pounded, and she again reached out to grasp Jacq's hand for comfort. He squeezed her hand firmly; his last goodbye, then the guard pulled them apart.

Jacq expected a guilty verdict for his crime of murder and was convinced he would be accused of theft and treason. He expected to be dead soon. His knees felt weak and shaky as they walked across the courtyard. He wanted to call out to Nada to help them, but she just stared back and then she closed her eyes and laid her head on the guard's shoulder. She was shutting them out. A large, hard choking lump formed in his throat, knowing for certain that Nada would not help them.

For some reason sounds and smells intensified in their long walk towards the door. The smell of fish cooking wafted to him on the breeze, gagged him. He could smell his sweat, the smell of fear. He could even smell the hot cobblestones, baking in the sun as they walked across them. This last walk seemed like an eternity.

Jacq thought of his first meeting with Carlotte. He cared for her. The loss of Carlotte alone was almost too much to bear. He shook his head to rid himself of any pleasant thoughts. He wanted to forget. He looked over at her and she whispered, "I love you Jacq." At any other time, those words would have made him the happiest man in the world, but he couldn't feel anything with this weight of sadness resting so heavy on his shoulders. Those words made the pain in his chest tighten even more.

When they reached the huge doors of the Hall of Justice the soldiers unceremoniously dragged them through. The sounds of their boots echoed on the polished white stone floor. The coolness of the tiles felt good on Jacq's injured feet. It seemed odd to experience this small pleasure.

Out of habit Jacq scanned for an avenue of escape. The guards had not shackled them, but he knew there was no point in struggling, no point in trying to escape. There was no escape for either of them.

CHAPTER 19

The movement of the soldier's body as he carried Nada across the antechamber felt strangely comforting and then she heard the huge doors open behind them and the scuffling footsteps of people entering. She knew without looking Jacq and Carlotte had just entered the building. A deep sadness again prevailed over all other thoughts. She felt wretched. A small voice told her she should be helping Jacq and Carlotte, but another voice told her she should be angry and make them all pay for stealing from her the only life she knew. Nothing would ever be the same for her again. The more she thought on this the angrier she felt. The guard again sensed her emotion and he patted her back as he carried her along.

"You are safe, Nada, nothing can hurt you now," he said.

He didn't realize the hurt had already taken place, having been abandoned by the only mother she knew. She just wanted to be left alone. She didn't want to speak with anyone.

The guard stopped and tapped lightly on a door. A familiar voice inside called for them to enter. The soldier entered the room and set Nada down on a large couch. He nodded to Nada who finally looked up into his face. He was young, not much older than Philen. He had a kind face. He smiled briefly at her then saluted Jorian.

"Your report later, Liam."

"Sir," he nodded and placed his fist on his heart in salute then quietly closed the door behind him.

Jorian gazed across the desk at Nada; the wild girl who played in the courtyard dust with the other children. He could not see her as someone of royal blood and would always think of her as he remembered her best, standing on a crate with a wooden sword, commanding her urchins to battle. He smiled at her, but no reciprocating smile or light of good humor broke the stoniness of her expression. She pulled her legs up onto the couch and wrapped her arms around her knees. She spoke not a word. A stab of fear touched Jorian's heart, she had only been missing a few days.

"Are you hurt, Nada?" Jorian asked, to get her talking, to find out as much as he could about the people who took her. "Did they hurt you?" He felt certain whatever occurred she would not make the discovery easy. "Did something scare you?" he said.

She shook her head no, in response.

"Did you eat today?"

She nodded that she had but again did not speak.

"Are you cold?"

She nodded yes so Jorian opened the cupboard behind his desk and took out a cloak which he draped across her shoulders.

"Is that better?" he asked.

She nodded and then her chin started to quiver. She hid face so Jorian could not see. The cloak smelled like Jorian; warm and comforting, like horses, dust and leather. Silent tears slid down her face, she felt so deeply and utterly unhappy.

"Why did you bring me here, Jorian?" she said into the wool of Jorian's cloak.

"I wanted to speak to you about the last few days, Nada. I need to find out about the people who took you and what they wanted. Can you tell me about them, the girl and the man, how did they take you?"

Nada looked up at him in surprise, "They didn't take me," she said.

"How did you come to be with them on the beach near the grotto if they didn't take you from your room?"

Nada explained everything that happened since Elieana left. When she talked about the man and woman with her that morning it was clear she thought well of them. This surprised Jorian, convinced they were involved in her kidnapping. Throughout the telling of her story Nada looked directly at Jorian, not taking her gaze off him. It rattled him that she did so. She seemed changed, older. It troubled him even more so when she told of the windowless room where her kidnapper kept her. What she had endured revealed to him the strength of her personality.

She told Jorian about Carlotte and Jacq, how they helped her escape from the house belonging to a man named Girard. Jorian knew that name well. He questioned her about Girard, but she could recall only when he came to her chamber; knocked Aldred down and held the putrid smelling cloth over her face. She remembered more about the soldier who brought her food and changed the bucket, but not enough to identify him.

When Nada told all she could tell, Jorian called a guard to escort her to the King's residence. Nada jumped up from the couch. Anger blazing red across her face. "Jorian, I do not belong in the residence of the King. I belong with Elieana." Her voice trembled, and she clenched her fists tightly at her sides. No more crying, she thought. No more crying she screamed at herself.

Jorian stepped around his desk, pulled her into his arms and hugged her close. He held her until she stopped shaking then gently pushed her back, still holding onto her arms. "Nada, you are a royal princess, you have always been a princess. You are Elieana's adopted daughter and will always be so to her. She loves you unconditionally. You are not losing Elieana; you are regaining a father who was broken with grief after losing you. You must return to him and renew your relationship with him as his only child and heir. But then you are not a child anymore, you are a young woman. Sixteen years, I think, are you not?"

Nada nodded sadly in acknowledgement of her failed celebration.

Jorian's grip then tightened on her arms as he thought of the upcoming wedding and the treaty signing, both brought danger to Nada. What would the King's adopted son do, when he discovered he could no longer be declared first in line to the Baltican throne? Nada squirmed to get him to release his hold on her.

“Jorian you’re hurting my arms,” she said as she struggled from his grip.

“Oh, I’m sorry Nada,” he said, and he released her, guiltily eying the tiny fingerprint bruises he made on her arms.

A tapping at the door heralded the arrival of Nada’s escort and she anxiously blurted out, “What will happen to Carlotte and Jacq? I want to help them as they helped me, Jorian. Please promise me you won’t let anything bad happen to them."

“I will do what I can Nada,” replied Jorian as he walked her to the door.

Liam, the same guard who brought her to Jorian stood outside and a covered palanquin and two men in plain livery stood beside it. Nada hesitantly climbed in. Liam ensured the curtains were tightly closed and then they left the Hall of Justice to the rooms set aside for Nada in the King’s residence.

The palanquin was soft and comfortable; richly decorated with carved wood and heavily embroidered cushions and curtains. It smelled of cedar, tangy and fresh. At any other time, Nada might have enjoyed the ride, but she couldn’t relax and sat stiffly upright. She propped herself up with her hands behind her, so she wouldn’t fall back onto the cushions. Occasionally she peeked out to see where they were but then quickly closed the curtain again as people in the streets stared back, curious to catch a glimpse of who might be inside.

Preparations for the upcoming wedding were well underway and anything unusual was bound to attract people’s attention. It wasn’t unusual then for people to stand and watch. Arturo, Girard’s second in command stood in the shadow of a building as the palanquin passed by. That morning his men reported the arrest of Jacq, Carlotte and the girl. Arturo proceeded to the Hall of Justice himself, to confirm their arrest. As he watched Jacq being escorted into the building he knew they had a short window of time before the King's men pounded on Girard's door. Girard, his identity kept secret all this time, to move freely throughout Pelagos, would not have his identity revealed because of the stupid gong farmer. Arturo took a small token out of the pouch on his belt. He stopped a young boy on the street and told him if he delivered the token he would be paid handsomely. The token, a signal to Girard; he must leave the city as soon as possible.

Arturo expected Jacq to spend a long, long time in the dungeon, but he waited to see if he would come out again, leading soldiers to Girard's house. When the palanquin came out instead, headed towards the King's residence, he hastily returned to Girard's house where Girard had already gathered up his most important possessions for their immediate departure.

"Tell the men to leave in small groups or singly. We will meet outside the wall an hour's ride from the city. Put Druce in charge of the encampment," Girard told Arturo when he returned.

"You and I will stay behind, to complete some unfinished business."

Arturo nodded then left to give direction to Girard's men, returning a short time later to assist Girard. They packed his valuables onto their horses then they parted company, each with their own errands to attend to before leaving.

Questioning of Jacq and Carlotte took the rest of the day and by the time the King's soldiers approached the house of Girard it had already stood vacant for five hours. The house stood dark and cold, the servants long since dismissed. The windows in Girard's study hung open and a breeze blew through the room scattering discarded papers across the floor. A pail of burnt ash all that remained of anything traceable to Girard.

Before leaving the city, Girard attended at a small house on a narrow street. He knocked on the door and a young woman peered out at him. He passed her a note then left as suddenly as he had arrived.

Mathilde's brothel was on the opposite side of the city. Girard held no loyalty to her. She was a liability and of no further use. Mathilde knew Arturo well, she did not ask any questions when he came to see her, swarthy and handsome, exuding danger which intensely appealed to her.

The flash of a knife, a slight exhalation of breath, her eyes widened in surprise, she slumped to the floor, crimson blood staining the front of her white robe. Arturo left silently and within moments blended in with the citizens in the crowded streets.

Dressed as a minor merchant Girard departed through the city gates and the great outer wall beyond and rode to his encampment beside the Kofathi where a hearty meal awaited him. The encampment had the appearance of a rich nobleman traveling to the city for the wedding. No one would question its presence and by the time anyone did, it would be much too late.

By the time Mathilde's maid discovered her lifeless body, Girard was toasting himself with a glass of sweet Baltican wine, the color of blood. The maid, upon finding Mathilde, dead eyes staring accusingly at her, ran screaming from the house with her apron covering her face.

Chapter 20

The cell stank of musty straw, urine and other repugnant odors. Carlotte sat silently in a corner staring at the bars to the cell, the cell even smaller than her room in Mathilde's brothel. She cried a little when the door slammed shut, the sound reverberating off the stone walls, but then she stopped, realizing tears changed nothing. She wrapped her arms around herself, shivering uncontrollably. The damp, dark stones of the walls gave off a chill that seeped into her bones making her feel brittle, as if she might shatter into thousands of tiny pieces.

A torch in a sconce hanging on the wall outside her cell gave off a somewhat comforting but foul-smelling light. She stood and paced back and forth, her shoes clicking on the flagstone floor as she rubbed her arms vigorously to warm herself.

She hadn't seen Jacq since the soldiers separated them and wondered how he had fared during the questioning. She thought about Nada, would she even bother to help them or forget? Sadly, she believed Nada would not help and then berated herself for mistrusting her.

Her thoughts moved again to Jacq and all that happened since they met. Was it only a few days ago? She felt scattered and frayed and couldn't think properly. The more she thought the more agitated she became. She shook her head to dislodge these feelings and how he had changed her life.

Mathilde would be furious. Every time she heard the guards moving around outside the cells she shivered with fear at the prospect of them taking her back to the brothel. Even more frightening, maybe Mathilde would come herself. Carlotte conjured a vision of Mathilde standing on the other side of the bars, her scowling face, her intense, dark eyes and long black hair that seemed alive when she spoke. She would look down her nose and say something hateful. These thoughts made Carlotte angry and she started to shiver violently.

Carlotte's short life, so full of unfortunate events that led her to be imprisoned but none of them were her own doing except these most recent events. Her merchant father and mother traveled a great deal. On one of those trips her parents died in an accident leaving her very much alone. She thought her aunt and uncle would take her into their home, even if only to live as a servant. She did not expect them to move into her parent's home and send her away.

Wistfully she imagined her parent's beautiful home in Girona, not large but comfortable. Behind the house a large courtyard overflowed with trees and shrubs and in the center a huge Manga tree gave them shade. Many a day she sat in the shade of the tree eating the delicious, manga fruit. She could almost taste its sweetness, feel the heat of the flagstones on her feet and smell the sweetly scented air.

Carlotte wondered if her aunt enjoyed the fruit after they sent her to Pelagos to live with Mathilde. They told her they were taking her to school in Pelagos but when she arrived Mathilde cruelly informed her there was no school but indenture as a servant. She wondered if her aunt and uncle really knew or cared what kind of a woman Mathilde was. "They probably knew exactly what kind of a woman Mathilde was," whispered Carlotte angrily, kicking the bars of the cell as hard as he could.

Carlotte's aunt hated Carlotte's mother, even though they were sisters, very different sisters indeed. Carlotte's mother, fair and kind and her aunt, Murtha, ungainly and mean spirited. She sighed deeply then fixed her mind to other things, feeling very sad but very angry at the same time. "There must be some way I can get out of this dungeon," she said out loud. "I cannot just stay here thinking about the past. Perhaps the guard will take a message to Nada. Guard, guard," she called out. "I need your help. Please come here. Please come and talk to me."

The sound of metal cup banged, and a bench scraped across the flags as an irate voice shouted out. "This better be important. Prisoners should be quiet in their cells." A big, oafish-looking man walked towards her cell. A yellowish slop of food stained the front of his once white shirt. Carlotte choked back the gagging feeling in her throat as she looked at him. He grasped the bars and leered at her. "What do you want," he sneered as he reached in and grabbed the front of Carlotte's dress, pulling her towards him.

His breath smelled of rotted meat and the bile rose in her throat as she replied, "I... I want to get a message to Nada," she stammered. She tried to push the man's hands away, his grip on the neck of her dress choking her.

"You're choking me," she croaked.

"I don't know who Nada is and if you want to send a message you'll have to pay. What do you have to give me?" he said as he loosened his grip and shook her.

"I don't have anything," she cried out. She grasped his hands again, trying to pull them away but he held on tight. She retched again from his stench. He pulled her towards him, bumping her face painfully on the bars of the cell.

The pain in her face immediately swept away her sadness, replaced with anger so palpable her whole body tingled. The man's eyes widened in surprise at the sudden change in her expression. She pulled and pulled, trying to get out of his grasp but he held on tightly. He waggled his tongue at her then grabbed her breast, pinched it painfully and ripped her dress.

"Let go of me," she screamed into his face.

"I'll let go of you after I'm done with you," he growled as he reached for the ring of keys hanging on his belt.

Carlotte's fear and anger bubbled like boiling water. Her thoughts centered on the guard. A tingling sensation traveled up the back of her neck causing the hair to rise on the top of her head. It ran down her back and down both arms. Heat spread throughout her whole body tingling every nerve. Her mother and father warned her of these feelings. They trained her to control them. Strange things happened when she concentrated on her anger. This time she would not control it. This time she would get what she wanted. She did not belong here, neither did Jacq. She wanted out. The feeling shrieked inside her head as if it were a living entity.

She looked at the guard with repugnance, his pock-marked face, his thick, rubbery looking lips, his foul-smelling breath, suddenly power surged throughout her body. Carlotte embraced the sensation. She let it flow through her body. Her fingers tingled. The bubbling sensation felt as if something inside her was trying desperately to escape. She felt an immense surge all around her as if a heavy wind blew through the cell. A rending screech of metal on metal echoed off the walls and then the cell door burst open. The keys flew from the guard's hand and his body slammed against the wall with a loud, meaty thump.

The guard lay rigid on the floor, staring back at her, white-faced with fear. Later he would tell his comrades the room became hot just for a second and then the prisoner vanished in a puff of smoke. He would never tell them what really happened, that she overpowered him with strength enough to slam him against the wall.

Carlotte walked out of the cell, not taking her eyes off the guard as she bent down and picked up the keys. "I am leaving now," she said, her voice quivering with surprise and awe and sounding as if it came from somewhere a long way off. She felt as if she hovered near the ceiling, observing everything below her.

The guard rolled over onto his belly and attempted to get up on his knees. He fell onto his face and then pulled himself up, holding onto the stones of the wall for support. He looked back just once; fear engraved on his face, his nose bloody from the fall and then he staggered down the passageway as fast as he could go.

Carlotte ran to Jacq's cell, startling him. He hadn't seen what happened but heard the commotion. She fumbled with the keys until she found the right one and unlocked the door.

Jacq asked in a high-pitched squeak, "What have you done?" and he backed away from her. "Why did the guard run away from you? Why did you scream?"

"I wanted to get out of there," she said, her voice loud in her ears. "I did not want to stay any longer. The cell door opened. I took the keys and now we can escape," she said, not wanting to tell him how, exactly, she got the keys. Still surprised herself, she couldn't explain what happened.

"What are you, Carlotte?" stammered Jacq fearfully, not altogether sure he wanted to know the answer. He heard stories of people who could make things happen, mystical, strange things. He didn't want to be associated with anyone who could do those things.

"Jacq, I am from Girona, my father was a merchant and well respected. I was their only child and when they died my aunt and uncle sent me away and took their house. I didn't realize, until this moment, why they sent me away. There was no love lost between my mother and my aunt, but I must have frightened my aunt and uncle very badly with what happens when I am angry." Her eyes stung as she thought of her lost family.

Jacq looked at Carlotte warily and then he thought about all they had been through in the few days they had known each other. She had helped him when she recognized he had a need and she fulfilled that need without question. Considering all that she had done for him he at least could give her his friendship and support. He reached out to her tentatively, as if he expected to receive a shock or something more dangerous then he grasped her hand and walked out of the cell. "Carlotte, I am sorry. I didn't know what to think when you walked...when you just did what you did."

Carlotte's mouth became a thin line. "I am not a freak," she said, "But we have to hurry, Jacq. We can talk later when we are far away from here."

Jacq nodded, thankful that the conversation was at an end. "Let's go then, I think I can find a way out," he said and pulled her further along the passageway.

"We must hurry; the guard will be back when he regains his courage," said Carlotte as she ran beside him. "I don't want to wait to find out what the guard will do to me when he returns," remembering that what she did might once have been acceptable in Girona but not in Pelagos. She hadn't done anything strange for such a long time and really didn't know how it was that she achieved the feat of destroying the lock on the cell door and knocking the man down. The look on Jacq's face made her realize that if he had any plans to leave her behind he now had a very good reason.

"I have been here before when I first started working as a gong farmer," said Jacq as they ran down the passageway. "There is a small door, locked from this side, leading to the sewers. I came here every morning to empty the slop buckets. We can get out through there and hopefully well away before the guard returns."

As they ran past the other cells the prisoners shouted, demanding to be set free. When they didn't stop, the prisoner's curses followed them to the end of the passageway. Another enemy, thought Jacq. He spied the refuse door; above it hung the key. Jacq's hands shook as he unlocked the door. He pushed it open and a fetid smell wafted out making him feel instantly nauseous. Fighting the feeling down he glanced at Carlotte. Her faced paled as she looked inside and then she pulled up the hem of her skirt and pinched her nostrils shut.

Tears welled up in Carlotte's eyes, making Jacq think the thought of going back into the sewers made her cry but then she whispered, "Jacq, I am sorry for what I did to the guard. I am sorry for scaring you. Thank you for helping me."

Jacq reached up, touched Carlotte's face and said, in a slightly squeaky, nervous voice, "Carlotte, I am sorry as well. I want to be your friend. You and I have relied on each other so much in the past few days. I would be lost without you."

A soft smile touched Carlotte's lips. "I want to be your friend too, Jacq. Let us leave Pelagos and find somewhere we both will be safe, safe to be ourselves without interference from others."

The sound of angry voices interrupted them. Jacq's eyes sprung wide open and he motioned for Carlotte to step through the opening. "Quickly, we must get away, they will know we escaped this way from the smell alone."

Carlotte climbed into the foul-smelling tunnel, keeping the hem of her dress pressed tightly against her face, Jacq close on her heels. They had just made it around a bend in the tunnel when they heard the door open and the guards arguing who would follow in pursuit. None followed, making Jacq giddy with relief. "You surely scared the guard out of his wits, Carlotte," Jacq laughed.

"I have never seen a guard run away before," she said.

Jacq laughed again as he led her away. The further they walked the further the fear of what happened there eased its way out of his mind. They were two of a kind, different and very unusual.

Chapter 21

Once again Carlotte found herself in the stinking tunnels under the city. Never in her wildest dreams would she have believed she would escape not once but three times, by this route. Her throat tightened as she gagged and held the cloth of her dress tightly over her face, as she tried to breathe. It helped a bit, but she could feel herself getting sweaty and knew in moments, if she did not get out of there, she would leave her breakfast in the tunnel. Carlotte laughed out loud, she didn't have any breakfast. In fact, she couldn't remember the last time she did have something to eat. It struck her as odd she could laugh at a time like this and then it crossed her mind perhaps she might be getting hysterical.

Noticing her discomfort Jacq called back over his shoulder, "Breathe through your mouth, it will help. Take small breaths. You will be all right Carlotte, we are almost there."

They turned around a sharp bend, running down a different tunnel but back in the direction from which they came.

"We are going towards Girard's house," Jacq called back.

"No," squeaked out Carlotte. "We cannot go back there."

"No, I don't mean into Girard's house," he said. "There is another tunnel that will take us above the pits where the sewers empty into big wooden tubs for the fields."

"Oh," Carlotte mumbled through the cloth of her skirt before clamping her mouth shut. Even though Jacq told her she should breathe through her mouth, she could not, every time she tried she gagged. She held her breath as she ran behind him, taking quick panting breaths.

"There is a vent where we can climb out," Jacq called back over his shoulder. He didn't tell her of his concern the vent might be locked or rusted shut or, if anyone worked nearby, they would have to wait until dark.

When they finally reached the vent opening, Jacq pushed Carlotte up the ladder, so she could get a breath of fresh air. She breathed in gulps of cool, fresh air until she could breathe normally, compose herself and regain what dignity she could under the circumstances. She whispered to Jacq who stood below her, "Thank you, Jacq, I don't think I could have gone much longer."

"I understand, Carlotte. No need for thanks," said Jacq, through his gritted teeth, trying not to breathe to deeply. "Can you come back down here so I can open the hatch?"

Carlotte climbed back down the ladder to change places with Jacq. At the bottom of the ladder she could still breathe, if somewhat shallowly, the fresh air flowing down from the vent, but she waited anxiously, hopping from foot to foot, while Jacq opened the hatch. "Will we be leaving soon? Is there anyone out there?" whispered Carlotte. "Jacq, are there people about? Will we have to wait, or can we soon leave here?" Becoming frantic, she rocked back and forth on her feet. Her flesh crawled with the thought of where they were and as if some unclean thing was wrapping itself around her.

Jacq climbed back down the ladder, a look of annoyance on his face. "There is someone outside standing by the tubs. He is not a guard; he looks like a farmer. I can't open the vent until he leaves."

"Yes," she replied quietly then clamped her mouth shut again and she pulled her skirt up over her mouth and nose. Carlotte's stomach churned, nothing could be done to change their situation now. She stood at the bottom of the ladder, loath to touch anything. She couldn't sit, and she didn't want to lean on the slime ridden walls, so she just stood in one place, weaving slightly and feeling increasingly unwell.

Jacq climbed back up the ladder then whispered, "Someone has come and is speaking to the farmer." As Jacq watched the two men, the farmer became agitated, waving his arms. Jacq could hear the man's voice raised in anger, but he could not make out the words. "They are arguing," whispered Jacq.

The other man stood quietly as the farmer expressed his anger then suddenly the other man pulled out a knife and plunged it into the farmer's abdomen. The farmer grunted in pain when the other man pulled the bloody knife out and wiped it clean on the back of the farmer's tunic. Slowly the farmer sank to his knees, clutching his abdomen. The other man lifted his foot, as if he didn't want to dirty his hands, and pushed the man down onto the ground. With nod of his head to the dying man he walked away and disappeared into the shadows.

"He stabbed him," Jacq whispered loudly, frantically. He slid down the ladder almost falling in a heap at the bottom. "He stabbed him and just walked away," Jacq said. Agitated, he ran his fingers through is hair making it stick up crazily then he ran back up the ladder to look out again.

Jacq waited a bit longer to ensure the stranger did not return then he started to push and pull on the lever to open the hatch until it gave way with a rusty, rasping screech. "Carlotte," he whispered, "We can climb out now I think it is safe."

Hearing Carlotte stirring below, he climbed out the vent opening so he could help her from the top of the ladder. Carlotte let out a gasp as soon as her head popped out in the open air. Jacq realized she must have been holding her breath. Her body shuddered in relief when she climbed fully out of the hatch and sank down onto the ledge.

"Carlotte, if your legs are not too cramped we need to get off this ledge. I am afraid someone may come. If the killer returns he may see us up here."

She grasped his outstretched hand and let him pull her to her feet. "Do you think the farmer is alive? Can we help him?" she whispered to Jacq before they started to climb down.

"I hope so. Hurry," replied Jacq as he grasped the top rail of the rusty ladder and climbed down.

Carlotte tucked her skirt up to keep it from tangling in her feet then followed Jacq down the ladder. When they reached the bottom, they hurried around the back of the huge vats to where Jacq saw the farmer fall and approached him cautiously. He lay on the ground, writhing in pain, unaware they approached until they stood beside him. He grunted at them, clenching his teeth as a wave of pain convulsed his body.

Carlotte bent down and smoothed the hair back off the man's face. Not a young face, one with heavy lines carved into it, showing hard years spent outside toiling in the fields. She took one of his gnarled, work-roughened hands and held it tightly. "Who did this to you?" she asked.

"Art... Art", he said but started to choke.

"Do you have a family where we can we take you?" she asked. The man moaned, arching his back in pain then shook his head that he did not.

"Where is your house we will take you to your bed and bring a healer?" His looked wildly around and grasped Carlotte's arm, his fingers digging into the soft flesh.

"House...third one...cart behind tubs," he choked out. "Take me to house. No healer," he grunted between clenched, bloodied teeth. He fell silent then, staring up to the heavens. At first Carlotte thought he died but she leaned down and felt the faint, fluttering of his breath on her cheek.

Jacq ran to retrieve the man's cart from behind the tubs. He found a dilhaa harnessed to the cart, its head hanging low, its nose almost touching the ground, sleeping soundly. Jacq pulled on its bridle and the animal snuffled and snorted, pawing at the ground unhappy to be woken from his slumber. The animal stubbornly planted its feet and would not move. Frustrated with the creature Jacq yanked hard on the bridle causing the beast to throw up its head in surprise. When he finally got it to move Jacq ran alongside the dilhaa, guiding it back to where the injured man lay.

Together Carlotte and Jacq helped the farmer stand and gently lay him in the cart. Jacq took the reins and drove the cart down the hard-packed road in search for the man's house, their path lit by what faint illumination the sliver of the moon provided.

Jacq needed comfort from what they just experienced but he also thought Carlotte did too, so he reached out to put his arm around her shoulders then pulled back. With a man dying in the back of the cart how could he even think of anything but getting the man to his home, his bed, so he could die in peace? Jacq sighed deeply then flicked the reins over the dilhaa's back.

They eliminated the houses as they passed, searching for the third house. The man said he had no family. In the third house, its occupants sat eating their evening meal. They drove the dilhaa to the end of the road without finding the house they sought. Anxiously Jacq turned the cart down a narrow lane until they came to three shacks in a row. The third one, dark and unoccupied, seemed to be the one so Jacq drove the cart into the front yard.

He jumped down and tied the dilhaa to the rickety railing surrounding the front porch as Carlotte opened the door of the shack. They assisted the man out of the cart and helped him inside. As they walked Carlotte noticed he seemed to get lighter, as if he already started to leave his body. When they got inside they laid him down on a rickety, narrow bed.

Carlotte lit a lamp and looked around the dimly lit shack. There were no comforts of a home. It seemed like a shelter only, to come from the fields, eat his evening meal and then sleep until he returned to his toil the next day. She filled a basin with stale water. A cloth she found hanging from a hook on the wall which she used to bathe the man's face. He smiled up at her in thanks, his mouth and teeth stained with blood. She realized he would not be long with them. She moved to leave him, but he grasped her arm and bade her to stay.

"Please," he rasped, "I must tell you, so you will help. I have made a grave mistake. My greed has brought me to this place where I die. You must take me toward Girona. You will find my family. My family will know," he choked on the words, "They will find you."

"I am from Girona, sir, I came to Pelagos as an indentured servant, my aunt and uncle sent me here. I do not know if I can go back there."

"You must go to Girona...," he choked and stumbled on his words and could not speak for some moments. "You must go towards Girona, for your own safety. I have let the wolf know of the weak places in the city, there will be an attack soon, very soon," again, the man choked and coughed.

Jacq came and stood behind Carlotte. She turned to face him, desperately wanting him to wrap her in his arms. He could see the sadness on her face, he wanted to help but panic threatened to overwhelm him. "Carlotte, we should leave here?" whispered Jacq, so nervous he started pacing back and forth, running his fingers through his hair. "The man will die; we cannot be caught here in this house."

"Jacq, we cannot leave," she whispered, "This man is my countryman. He is from Girona. He cannot die here alone." She flopped down on the floor beside the bed and took the man's rough, work-worn hand in hers and gently stroked it.

Apprehensively Jacq accepted this but crossed his arms across his chest to stop himself from shaking. The man spoke again, his breath raspy and so quiet they had to lean over him to hear what he said. "You must leave the city. There will be an attack on Pelagos. Leave or die. There is gold in a hole under the bed. Take it. I ask only that you take my body towards Girona." The man groaned, arching his back, in agony. He ground his teeth, twisted his body with the pain, breathed in one long, rasping, rattling breath then he died.

Carlotte and Jacq looked at each other, both stricken with the shock of the death of this man. They did not even know his name. Silent tears rolled down Carlotte's cheeks as Jacq gently shut the man's eyes and pulled the coverlet over his face. Jacq crouched down beside Carlotte and stroked her hair. "Carlotte, we don't know this man, how can you be so touched by his death?" he asked, very innocently.

Carlotte realized Jacq must not have known a family as she had and would not feel the same towards death as she did. "Jacq, I mourn for what will never be. I weep for his children, or the grandchildren who will never know him. I lament for his wife, for her loss; for us because we have lost a friend. We must carry out his wish, take him back to his home, to Girona."

From the determined look upon Carlotte's face Jacq realized he could do nothing but fulfill the man's dying request. He didn't know how to get to Girona. He had never been outside of the city walls in his life and hoped Carlotte could guide them to the right road. With a sudden pang of fear, he realized for the first time in his life he was leaving this city, perhaps for good. He stood then and reached out to Carlotte. She rose from the chair, letting him wrap his arms around her. He held her tightly, hoping to give her some comfort but also to receive comfort from her as he held her in his arms. She rested her head upon his shoulder, allowing herself one moment of solace from this man she hardly knew. They embraced for a long time then Carlotte gently pushed him back, leaned her head to one side and gazed down sadly at the body of the man on the bed.

"I will clean his body before we leave, will you help me?" asked Carlotte?

Jacq fought the urge to say no and nodded. He helped Carlotte cut off the man's bloodied clothing then burned it in the stove. Carlotte cleaned away the blood from the man's body and face. She pressed a thick pad of cloth over his wound, tying it tightly in place with a strip she tore off a blanket. They dressed him in the only other set of clothes they found, barely worn, perhaps kept for special occasions. From the lack of wear, the man probably didn't have many special occasions.

Upon completing their task, they searched the hut for anything identifying the man. In the hole beneath his bed they found it, the small bag of gold, a small book and papers important enough hide and a few small trinkets. Jacq flipped through the book and as he did, his hands shook. Recorded on the pages were all the man's dealings with Girard and any of the other men in Girard's employ. Jacq felt a sudden satisfaction. He had been right about Girard being involved. The last entry in the little book recorded a meeting he would have with a man named Arturo. Carlotte and Jacq looked at each other, both realizing what they held. If Girard or Arturo knew of the existence of the book and that Jacq and Carlotte possessed it, they would not be long for this world.

Before, Jacq would have gone straight to Girard, handed the book over to him, expecting a reward of some kind, but now he knew death was the only reward Girard would grant him. He silently vowed Girard would never see this book until he stood in front of the Supreme Justice of Pelagos. Jacq closed the book and placed it back into the box with the rest of the man's possessions.

They found enough supplies in the shack to last them on their journey to Girona. They loaded the cart with the rations, the box of possessions and the farmer's body, covered with blankets. Jacq sat in the cart waiting for Carlotte to climb aboard when she ran back into the shack.

"What were you doing?" asked Jacq when she returned and climbed up onto the wagon seat beside him.

"I wrote a note to say he left to go to his home in Girona."

"But what if the killer comes back looking for him?" said Jacq. "He will see the note and know someone else wrote it. He will follow."

"The only way he could have written the note, Jacq, is if he wrote it before they met. The man killed the farmer and knew it when he left him lying in the dirt. We are safe, I am sure of it. We will come to no harm from the killer," said Carlotte. She smiled at him then sat up straight with her hands folded in her lap. "Let's go," she said, taking a deep steadying breath.

Jacq nodded, a troubled look flitted across his face then he flicked the reins and steered the dilhaa out onto the narrow track leading from the village. The sliver of moon, now obscured by clouds, gave them little light to see by so he relied on the dilhaa to stay on the track as they headed towards their freedom. Thankful for the night's inky darkness they believed anyone who saw them leave could not describe them to the authorities in any event.

"I think we can go some distance towards the main gate and then pull off to wait until it is open at sunrise," said Carlotte.

"How do you know this?" asked Jacq.

"I recall, when my aunt and uncle brought me here, we arrived too late to enter. We camped outside the wall until morning. The gates open at sunrise and close at sunset. I remember my aunt being very angry. She could not be rid of me fast enough. The whole time we traveled from Girona I had to sleep under the wagon. It frightened me so much to be alone I had a hard time controlling my thoughts. Throughout the trip, on those dark nights alone, my thoughts made things move and bang against the sides of the wagon. My aunt screamed at me to stop. She threatened to beat me. During the night, I listened to her telling my uncle how happy she would be when we reached Pelagos and she could leave me there."

Carlotte became silent, brooding over past events. Wisely Jacq didn't ask any further questions.

Soon the narrow track met with the wider road leading to the outer walls of Pelagos. Jacq drove the cart onto the road and they traveled until they found a place, behind a large tree a short distance from the road, where they could pull off until morning.

"I'll cut some branches to hide the cart," said Jacq as he jumped down. "If Arturo is on the road we don't want to take the chance he will come to ask for food or drink."

"Yes, Jacq, you are right. I have spoken to Arturo before at Mathilde's house. He will know me also."

Carlotte unharnessed the dilhaa, hobbling him so he could not run off while Jacq cut branches and laid them against the cart, concealing it. After he finished he walked a good distance away from the cart before lying down. Carlotte followed him to the spot he chose and lay down beside him. She knew they need not be concerned about wild animals on this side of the wall. The man's body, well covered by the blankets, deterred birds and other small animals.

"I'm not a superstitious man, Carlotte, but I fear the farmer's spirit will follow us, maybe to be sure we carry out his last wishes." He didn't look at Carlotte because he felt a bit silly when he voiced his concern, but he needed to say it nonetheless. He didn't want to be silent and then have unexplained things happen to them. Carlotte patted his arm and then a few seconds later Jacq could hear her slow, steady, breathing, of a much-deserved deep sleep.

Jacq, being so nervous, slept little, not only because Arturo might have seen them leave but also because of the dead farmer in the back of the cart. First light brightened the sky in what seemed just a few moments. Carlotte awoke to find Jacq leaning against the tree looking at her out of red rimmed eyes. Realizing he had not slept at all she said nothing to him. From his comments the evening before, about spirits following them, and his reaction to sleeping nearby the cart she didn't want to pursue the subject.

The day promised to be sunny and warm with easy travel on the hard-packed, dirt road to Girona. They hitched the dilhaa to the cart and climbed up, neither saying much of anything. Carlotte rooted around in the sack of food they took from the farmer's shack and produced a loaf of stale bread and overripe fruit. "Odd," said Carlotte, as she munched on the tough, stale bread. "It seems a long time ago you first came to Mathilde's. So much has happened in the last few days."

Jacq grunted but said nothing.

"Do you think the villagers have looked for the farmer?" asked Carlotte.

Again, Jacq grunted then replied, "I think not. He seemed like a solitary man. Even so, I think his disappearance and death will be twisted around so I am blamed," he said grumpily.

"You worry too much, Jacq," replied Carlotte. "Pelagos is a huge city and the soldiers will think we have hidden there. Besides, there is no body and we left a note. Why would anyone look for someone who left a note to tell where he went?”

"Well what about all the blood by the tub?" said Jacq, trying to beat down her cheerfulness.

"They will think something like a dog killed a small animal and carried it off," she replied.

“I am worried about the note,” he said. “If they are looking for the farmer don’t you think they will look by the gates to question him? And if it is the man who murdered him don’t you think he will find the note as well and be looking for him?”

Jacq refused to let the issue drop. Carlotte shook her head, a look of frustration passing across her face.

"Jacq, you worry about things over which you have no control."

Jacq huffed and fell silent, having seen the look on her face before she hid it and then the sound of hoof beats approaching interrupted their discussion. They peered through the shrubbery to see the King’s men galloping past.

“You don’t suppose they are looking for us, do you?” asked Jacq with a tremor in his voice.

“I hope not. If they find us with the farmer in the cart we will have little chance to explain what happened before we are put back in the dungeon. No one will believe us; the story is too incredible. I think perhaps we should wait until later in the day when more people are on the road.”

Jacq agreed, and they unhitched the dilhaa, tying it to a tree so it could graze.

"Jacq, what if we gather wood to put on top of the body. If we are stopped and they question us we can tell the guards, it is to make furniture and we are taking it to my uncle in Girona."

"I think that is a good idea," said Jacq. "The wood will keep any birds off the body as well."

He set about cutting long, slender sapling branches while Carlotte loaded them onto the cart. They waited throughout the morning until the sun shone high in the sky then again hitched up the dilhaa and drove the cart back onto the road. Only a few travelers were heading towards the gates to leave Pelagos, more entered, on their way to the city for the wedding. The guards searched the carts entering but ignored the ones leaving, giving Jacq and Carlotte only a cursory glance as the little cart laden with wood rattled past them. They both sighed with relief as they realized the guards at the gate probably had not received a warning to watch for two fugitives leaving through the outer gates. Their pursuers must believe they stayed in the city and the search for them would still be going on in earnest. On this, they were correct. Guards were stationed nearby the pathways leading to the shore from the Mermaid Tavern and from the farmer's village. If Jacq and Carlotte waited in the farmer's house, to leave at daylight, they would have been discovered as rapidly as before.

Guards walked in pairs throughout the city. Never had the people seen such a representation of the city's soldiery. By early morning the King's soldiers started a thorough search of the city, working their way slowly and methodically from house to house, starting in the poorest section. They found nothing, not the slightest trace of a great many people. Girard and his household and the two who escaped from the dungeons had vanished.

With trepidation Jacq and Carlotte drove the cart under the archway of the outer wall. Huge stone gargoyles crouched on ledges at the height of the arch, their mean, stone faces, glared down and Carlotte felt the urge to scream or run to escape their accusing, staring eyes. She had done no wrong but perhaps she had and didn't realize it, to feel so guilty. She clung onto Jacq's arm tightly, leaning against him, as they entered the tunnel and as they passed through the tunnel she saw guards standing in little alcoves watching them.

Carlotte guessed the tunnel to be twenty feet long and by the time they emerged into the warm sunshine on the opposite side she realized she had broken out into a cold sweat. The feeling of joy to be out in the open again, feeling the heat of the sun on her face, overwhelmed her like a giant bubble bursting out of her chest. She gave Jacq a quick hug, surprising him so thoroughly he fumbled the reins, causing the dilhaa to honk irritably. Before them stretched the ribbon of hard-packed road and for both the promise of a new life.

They proceeded at a quick pace for the dilhaa, each silent with their thoughts of life free from servitude. It did not seem to be as frightening as they both anticipated, outside the confines of the City of Pelagos. Although the city of Pelagos was one of great beauty, both Carlotte and Jacq knew only the ugly side of it and felt a great relief to be out in the wide-open country. Both feared wild animals with nothing to protect them except the axe they found in the farmer's shack but the fear of returning to the city far outweighed the fear of any animal.

With her thoughts on Girona Carlotte gazed unseeing at the road before them. Jacq, not knowing what to expect stared at the road ahead with trepidation. Neither of them spoke, the only sound, the Dilhaa's feet slapping on the ground as he pulled the cart further into the wilderness beyond Pelagos.

Carlotte didn't know exactly how to get to Girona, she only knew they had to go south and east and cross the Kofathi River. They passed no intersecting roads leading towards the river, so they traveled on, searching for a bridge to take them across or, by chance, some traveler on their way to the city to give them directions. By late afternoon they saw brightly colored flags waving from the tops of huge tents, nestled in amongst some tall trees between the road and the river. From the numbers of tethered horses, they guessed many armed men camped there. At first Jacq wanted to stop and ask the way until he saw the crest on the flag topping the largest tent, Girard's crest. Without a word, Jacq slapped the reins on the dilhaa's back, causing it to bleat in surprise.

A few men, standing nearby the road, glanced in their direction, their attention caught by the bleating of the dilhaa. None made a move towards them, they just watched the cart as it passed by the encampment. Jacq kept his head down and hunched his shoulders. He didn't recognize the men standing there but did not want to take the chance that they might recognize him. He knew that the smell of the sewer on his clothing might attract unwanted attention and slapped the reins on the dilhaa’s back again, getting it into a resistant joggling trot.

Anxious to stop and ask the way Carlotte huffed in annoyance at Jacq's sudden determination to push the beast faster. “Jacq, just stop for a moment, can’t you see the beast is almost worn out? Besides they may give us directions and a little something to eat.”

Jacq reached over and squeezed her arm, shaking his head, “It’s Girard,” he whispered.

Carlotte’s eyes grew round and her mouth opened as if to say something, but nothing came out. She immediately jumped down off the cart and patted and consoled the dilhaa as she trotted alongside it, gently pulling on its bridle, urging it on. The dilhaa stopped braying and obediently followed Carlotte.

Jacq surreptitiously looked back over his shoulder to see if anyone in the camp followed them. The men still watched them, and Jacq did not relax until they rounded a bend and could no longer see the tops of the tents over the trees. When they rounded the bend Carlotte jumped back into the cart without waiting for it to stop.

“That was frightening, Jacq,” whispered Carlotte as if she thought someone could hear her speaking.

“I know,” he murmured. Jacq didn't look at her; he just focused on the road ahead, trying to keep his hands from shaking. “Girard is not the man to cross. I don’t know what he planned to do with Nada, but I am glad she is safe now,” said Jacq.

“Do you think she tried to help us after they put us in the dungeon?” asked Carlotte.

“Hmmm, it’s hard to say,” replied Jacq, turning to face her. “We weren’t there long enough to find out, were we?” he grinned. “Thanks to you.”

A thought struck Jacq as he grinned at Carlotte. He had never really smiled much before he met her. Before, in his old life, he had nothing to smile about. He felt good and his face split into a huge grin.

“You’re welcome, Jacq,” said Carlotte. She laughed and squeezed his hand and they both sat, each in their own thoughts, smiling and happy for the first time in a very long, long time.

A short while later a little bridge came into view, leading across the river. A small, weathered signpost pointed towards the bridge, Kofathi River – Girona with an arrow pointing the way across the bridge. They crossed the bridge and when they reached the opposite side they unhitched the dilhaa and led him down to the river to drink. Carlotte filled their stone bottles and then splashed the refreshing water over her face.

"This feels so cool and fresh Jacq. Isn't it wonderful?" said Carlotte, forgetting her fear from the night before and upon seeing Girard's tents. She now eagerly anticipated their journey and gave a quick thanks to the Goddess they were at last away from Pelagos

Jacq squatted down beside her at the edge of the river, taking a moment to drink his fill of the cool river water. "I have never tasted any water so fresh and clean before," he said. "This is good." He wet his kerchief and wiped his face and neck. Thinking while he did it he never really took the time to clean himself until he met Carlotte. He felt somewhat embarrassed for the man he had been, and his heart swelled with love for this girl who changed his life.

Carlotte removed her shoes and socks, dangling her feet in the water. "I wish we could stop here for the rest of the day and bathe," she said, looking up at Jacq, smiling.

"It would be nice to stop but we should try and put as much distance as we can between ourselves and Girard's camp," said Jacq. "I do not want to meet up with any of his soldiers."

A look of shock crossed her face, wiping the smile away; she hadn't thought they might come this way or even follow them. "You are right; we cannot stop for a moment longer." She jumped up, grabbed her shoes and stockings in one hand and the dilhaa's bridle in the other and ran barefoot back up the hill, pulling the dilhaa along beside her.

Carlotte had the dilhaa hitched up and sat in the cart anxiously waiting for Jacq by the time he reached the top of the hill. He climbed into the seat beside her, took the reins and clicked his tongue. The dilhaa immediately started trotting as fast as it could go, sensing their anxiety.

After they traveled a goodly distance away from the river Jacq looked for a place they could pull off the road with enough shrubbery where they could hide the cart. He drove the cart behind some thick shrubs and un-harnessed the dilhaa, tying it with a long tether so it couldn't wander too far way. The beast immediately lay down and rolled over and over getting so completely tangled it couldn't get up. Carlotte giggled as it lay there helpless on the ground.

"The stupid beast," grumbled Jacq. "I have a mind to leave him lying there for being so stupid." Carlotte took pity on the dilhaa which she now called Clump for the way his feet slapped on the roadway. She untangled the dilhaa and the beast nuzzled her face as she patted it and scratched its ears, "I like you too, little Clump," she whispered and gave it a big hug, then she left him loose to wander and eat its fill of the lush grass in the clearing.

Carlotte rejoined Jacq where he sat in the cool shade of the trees. They ate a meager meal of stale bread and the remaining fruit, followed by the fresh, cold water from their stone bottles, so cold Jacq had an immediate headache. As soon as he drank it a pained expression spread across his face and he fell back into the thick moss under the tree, causing Carlotte to giggle with abandon. They stayed in the clearing, enjoying each other's company, for just a short while until they once again set out on the road to Girona. The sun beat down mercilessly and as the day wore on a distinctive odor, which couldn't be ignored, percolated from the back of the cart. They realized they needed to reach their destination soon or the farmer's burial place would be in the forest beside the road.

"What do you expect to find when you return to Girona?" Jacq asked after they had traveled in silence for some time.

Carlotte hesitated when she answered, "I don't know, it may be better if I don't go to my parent's...my aunt's house. There will be no warm welcome for me there."

"I think maybe we should find the farmer's family and from there we can decide to stay or go on to somewhere else, perhaps a village on the coast south of Girona?" said Jacq.

"Do you remember in the farmer's things, in all the letters, was there something with his name on it? I feel as if I am not being respectful by just calling him the farmer?" said Carlotte.

Jacq reached into his pocket and pulled out the bundle of papers from the farmer's possessions. In their haste, they did not look through them so as they rode along they carefully went through all the documents in the bundle. Some were letters, all to a person named Rodolph. They assumed Rodolph was the farmer's name. Suruchea, the person writing the letters pleaded for him to come home but the last, only a few neatly written lines told him not to return.

"I wonder who Suruchea is?" said Carlotte. "Do you think she might be his wife? How sad, if it is his wife and she has told him not to come home."

Jacq nodded, "Suruchea is an unusual name, perhaps it may not be difficult to find her. "It will be even sadder still when we bring him home," replied Jacq as he flicked the reins.

In that golden time of evening when the light of the setting sun made everything soft and comforting Jacq spotted a perfect place to pull off the road. A huge tree, its branches hanging down and sweeping the ground beneath, the perfect shelter for the night, hidden from anyone passing by on the road. They were stopping just in time for in the distance heavy dark clouds rolled in, threatening rain and, they hoped, bringing cooler temperatures. "We can sleep under the big tree over there, Carlotte. I will secure the cart a distance away while you make a place for us."

Carlotte nodded and jumped down from the cart and passed through the sweeping canopy of branches.

Afraid animals might be attracted to them because of the stink emanating from the cart Jacq pulled it under a smaller tree a short distance away from where they planned to sleep. He removed all the sticks piled on the corpse and packed dry spruce needles in around the body then replaced the sticks, retying them snuggly down on top. The pungent spruce needles masked the stink somewhat and, he hoped, enough to deter animals from coming to investigate during the night. When Jacq finished repacking the cart he went to the large tree and crawled in under the branches. The heavy, pungent smell of spruce permeated the air under the tree where Carlotte had scraped together a thick carpet of dry needles to make a soft, springy bed.

Jacq went back out and cut some boughs off a nearby maiden tree and wove a stiff matt under which they both could sleep; having never been in a forest before he was quite proud of this addition to their bed. When their bed was finished he led the dilhaa under the tree with them; they could not afford to lose the faithful little animal. He tethered the dilhaa to a branch with a huge pile of grass where it munched contentedly. Jacq and Carlotte finished their remaining food then crawled into the makeshift bed, snuggling together for warmth.

Plagued by nightmares, Jacq slept fitfully, rolling back and forth until Carlotte finally got up and walked to the outer branches of the tree. She stood quietly, breathing in the fresh air, a welcome change to the pungent spruce smell and gazed out at the sliver of the moon and the sky full of stars. The clouds, which previously threatened rain, had disappeared with the breeze that now caressed her face. As she stood looking out a tiny movement nearby the tree where they left the cart caught her eye. It looked like a swaying branch which seemed out of place then it dissolved from her vision.

She remembered her father telling her if she concentrated on seeing something in the dark she would not really be able to see it, so she shifted her gaze slightly to one side of what had attracted her attention. She saw it again, another movement, slow like something gliding from tree to tree, using the branches as cover in the dim moonlight. She saw other movements further away but this one seemed to be coming closer as it circled the clearing, staying close to the trees as it moved.

A tingling feeling ran up Carlotte's spine. She felt the prickling of her hair rising at the back of her neck. Carlotte stood completely still, not wanting to draw attention to herself. The creature went to the tree where Jacq left the cart. The sagging branches moved then lay still then moved again. The creature now walked directly towards where she stood. It had to cross a small spot where moonlight lit the ground in silver light. As the creature moved across the grass it changed from looking like moving greenery to the long silver tipped spears of grass. The creature wasn't thin like the grass, but it seemed as if the grass reflected from its body, so the bottom half looked like grass and the top as part of the trees in the background. Carlotte rubbed her eyes with her knuckles, trying to understand what she was looking at, her sleep-fogged brain could not comprehend it.

The two-legged creature had a slender body and long thin arms; its bare skin changed depending on what it stood close to. Carlotte tried to scream but nothing passed her lips. Her body tensed, and she stood frozen in place, watching, and then the creature looked directly at her. Its huge eyes widened in surprise as it met her gaze. They both stood staring at each other for some time then the creature walked closer. It stopped in front of her and stared into her face then slipped between the hanging boughs and stood beside her.

Trembling, Carlotte tried to will Jacq awake, wondering why he wouldn't wake up and if he did what would the creature do. After a few moments, the creature gracefully motioned for her to sit. Under the tree the creature's color faded to the background of the boughs hanging down behind it. Once Carlotte sank down to a seated position the creature sat down opposite her. The creature produced a small leather pouch and a small leathern dish, from where she could not tell, and placed a few small pieces of wood in the dish then produced a flint and started a fire using tiny sticks and needles it plucked from the ground.

Carlotte watched in wonder as a flame burned brightly on top of the little leather dish but did not burn it. The flame danced merrily as the creature fed it more bits and pieces of dried grass and twigs. Carlotte could now see the creature's face clearly and after a long silence it spoke to her. Its voice seemed a combination of the wind blowing in the trees and the gurgling of a stream. It sounded foreign and strange but as music to the ear.

"I don't understand what you are saying," said Carlotte.

The creature haltingly repeated back to her what she just said, making the words seem strangely beautiful.

"Why are you repeating me? Who are you? What do you want?"

Again, it repeated her words. Carlotte soon became frustrated and angry. The creature responded with a similar tone and mood. It suddenly dawned on her that the creature was a chameleon, taking on all the different attributes of what it touched or came close to. She wondered then if this creature could look like her. She reached over and very gently touched its arm, immediately the creature's skin started to change, taking on the appearance of Carlotte's skin where she touched it, but the rest of its arm remained grayish green like the tree. It looked as if she held a disembodied hand and she pulled back in alarm. Immediately the creature changed back to the grayish green texture of the tree boughs.

Carlotte looked up at the creature's face and suddenly felt the urge to laugh, probably from nervousness or the fact this creature was the most wondrous being she had ever seen. She doubted it had encountered many of her own kind. Humans were a superstitious, ignorant group. She felt certain if anyone knew these creatures existed they would be hunted and driven out of the land.

"Why are you here?" she asked.

"Why are you here?" it repeated.

She felt she could go on asking questions of this creature and have it repeat them forever, so she pointed to herself. "Carlotte," she said.

"Carlotte," it said and pointed at her.

She pointed at the creature but didn't say anything. The creature nodded, understanding what she wanted, and it pointed to itself, "Wirliang," it said. It pointed to Jacq and said "Carlotte?"

"No, no, Jacq," replied Carlotte. "Man," she added, pointing to Jacq, then pointed to herself, "woman."

The creature cocked its head to the side as if wondering how to respond then got up and moved towards the outer branches of the tree. The creature stuck its head out between the branches and let out a gurgling sound and a few seconds later pulled another smaller creature under the tree with them. The creature pointed to itself and said, "Man, Wirliang then pointed to the other creature and said "woman, Wirlean." The names, very similar, just meant man and woman.

The creatures amazed Carlotte, they remembered far more than she did with no difficulty at all. It must be, she thought, as chameleons they can mimic more than just a different appearance or their surroundings. It must be even the speech of others they can mimic as well. They talked for quite a long while until out in the distant forest they heard a loud roaring and snarling. Wirliang and Wirlean stiffened and then pulled Carlotte to her feet. They wanted her to leave immediately. Another of the creatures came in, untied the dilhaa and led it out from the shelter of the tree. More chameleon creatures came in and lifted Jacq from the sleeping pallet. He struggled for just a moment but then they sprinkled something on his face and he fell back asleep. As they lifted him their skin shimmered for a moment and then seemed to take on the appearance of the parts of Jacq's clothing they touched. They removed Jacq from under the hanging branches of the tree, leaving Wirliang and Carlotte standing alone, looking at each other. When she heard the animal snarling she didn’t want to leave the shelter of the tree. Wirliang reached over, his long fingers grasping her arm and changing color as they did so. He gave a slight tug on her arm and pointed in the direction the others went. Carlotte pushed the branches aside and stepped out into the clearing.

A few of the creatures stood near the cart. Others were already walking away from them, entering the forest on the opposite side of the clearing. This time they did not glide unseen from tree to tree. It looked odd. As they moved they looked like puddles of shimmering water drifting away from her. The ones carrying Jacq shimmered and changed as they moved, making it look as if Jacq floated away, into the trees, all by himself.

Initially Carlotte wanted to run away. She started to walk back towards the tree, to return to its pungent shelter but watching Jacq drifting away from her, overpowered her desire to flee, reminding her of her commitment to him. She followed the Wirliang through the forest, trying to keep Jacq in her sights, more afraid of losing him than where they were going.

They walked through the forest along a trail bounded on both sides with thick shrubbery, which at times obscured the trail completely. Eventually Carlotte could see the sky. The trees became fewer and father apart as they walked up a slight incline. They left the forest behind and climbed out onto a steep slope scattered with large boulders and rubble. The odd shadow and tumbling of pebbles disturbed by their feet the only indication she was accompanied by anyone or anything. At times, the cart seemed to float into the air as the creatures lifted it up and around obstacles. It disturbed Carlotte to follow behind Jacq who seemed to float up the hill as they carried him higher and higher.

When Jacq disappeared behind a large boulder Carlotte expected to see him come around the other side and climb higher still but he did not. Each Wirliang followed the other and did not reappear. She realized then there must be an entrance to a cave behind the boulder. It looked like just another huge boulder and had she been climbing in these hills by herself she would have missed the entrance altogether.

Carlotte rounded the boulder and saw the moonlight gilded entrance to a tunnel, the dilhaa and cart disappearing into its black maw. Carlotte felt Wirliang's hand on her shoulder pushing her forward into the bleak tunnel. She looked back at Wirliang with a feeling of foreboding, but she couldn't see him in the dark. When this is over, she swore silently to herself, I will never go into a tunnel or underground again.

The rich, loamy smell of earth scented the tunnel, a comforting smell linked to memories of her mother's garden at home, but the smell did nothing to comfort her. Carlotte looked back one more time to see the pale, rectangular entrance steadily shrinking in size. Her heart pounded. Tension and anxiety rose in her body causing her head to ache. Wirliang's hand never leaving her shoulder kept her from screaming aloud.

They walked on and on. The path seemed straight with a slight decline but at times moved to left and right. Carlotte dragged her fingers along the tunnel walls to keep a sense of balance. At times, she felt tree roots hanging down along the walls. Carlotte guessed the tunnel went around the roots so as not to disturb the tree above.

After a long period of walking downwards Carlotte noticed she could make out the shadowy shapes of the creatures walking in front of her and then she saw the opening into an enormous cavern. They stood high up on the cavern wall. From their vantage point she spied the Wirliang moving around below, on tiny roads, between small buildings. The cavern seemed to glow with a soft golden light. She gazed in wonder at the vastness of it. Carlotte looked back at Wirliang whose mouth drew back into a large, open mouthed smile, revealing rows of tiny, flat teeth. His color now a shimmering gold, the glowing, golden colored walls lending this new golden hue to their skins. They were beautiful.

She could see the Wirliang more easily in this light. Carlotte couldn't understand how they illuminated the cavern, she saw no torches, just a golden glow emanating from the walls and ceiling high overhead. A waterfall flowed from a hole in the cavern wall opposite them, filling a small lake below. The air was moist and fresh, and a slight mist rose up from where the waterfall tumbled into the lake.

The path down from the tunnel forked and somc of the Wirliang led the dilhaa and cart to the right. Many Wirliang lined the road and as the cart passed they slowly removed the sticks piled on top of the farmer's body. Probably they want the wood, she thought. At first, it seemed these creatures revered or treasured wood. She was partially right but when they emptied the cart of wood and only the body remained some of the larger Wirliang lifted the body gently out of the cart and carried it towards a building that looked very much like a temple. The Wirliang creatures who removed the sticks followed at the rear of the procession and lay the sticks back in the cart as they passed, chanting or singing as they followed the Wirliang carrying the farmer's body.

Odd, thought Carlotte, I wonder why they want the farmer's body. She turned to the Wirliang walking with her, "How did they know a body lay in the cart, aside from the smell, I mean? I promised him I would take him to his family." Bewildered and anxious Carlotte walked towards the temple but the Wirliang stopped her. He pointed to the left fork in the road leading to the lake and nudged her forward. Carlotte looked back over her shoulder towards the group of Wirliang and watched as the last of them entered the building.

When Carlotte and the Wirliang arrived at the water's edge she saw Jacq, sleeping soundly. The Wirliang motioned to a group of Wirlean, Carlotte assumed they were Wirlean because of their size. They approached and motioned Carlotte towards a building beside the lake. Curious, Carlotte walked towards the building. Inside the Wirlean started to remove her clothes. She struggled at first but then sniffing herself she realized she smelled quite foul and they wanted her to bathe. Carlotte allowed them to help her. They used fine sand to scrub her skin and washed her hair with scented soap. It felt luxurious, the very first time in her life someone had cared for her in this way.

When the Wirlean finished they wrapped her body in a soft, floor-length gown. The fabric shimmered and changed color with every movement. The Wirlean led Carlotte back to the spot where she last saw Jacq. Mats, pillows and soft blankets lay there now. Carlotte assumed that it was for her to rest and wait for Jacq and that they had taken him to bathe as well. She lay down, stretched with pleasure, feeling the warmth of the sand penetrating and warming her body. Her last waking thought, the sand is warm down here under the ground, and then she slipped into a deep, dreamless sleep.

Chapter 22

A small band of horsemen rode as quickly as they could down the road to Girona. Their livery identified them as Girard's house soldiers. They sought a cart loaded with wood, a man and a woman. The soldier who saw them pass by Girard's encampment earlier in the day did not recognize Jacq, but upon hearing some of his comrades discussing Jacq, the theft of Girard's money bag and Jacq's escape from the city he realized he had allowed an opportunity slip from his grasp. Girard offered a healthy reward for anyone bringing Jacq to him, alive.

Jacq and Carlotte had already camped under the tree when the soldiers first rode past. Jacq had hidden their presence well enough that they could not be seen from the road. When the soldiers again passed by Jacq and Carlotte's encampment the Wirliang had already paid their visit and were entering the tunnel to their underground cavern.

The soldiers, in their haste to collect Girard's healthy reward, had missed one clue, the tracks of the wheels of the cart where Jacq had pulled it off the road. When they returned the next day, they followed the cart tracks into the forest but were bewildered when the tracks disappeared completely. They found Jacq and Carlotte's encampment but all that remained, under the huge tree, was a leather dish with the ash of burnt twigs and needles upon it.

24286448R00125

Printed in Poland
by Amazon Fulfillment
Poland Sp. z o.o., Wrocław